FOR
TURON GOLD

DON DELANEY

Introduced by Tom Thompson

ETT IMPRINT

Exile Bay

Published by ETT Imprint, Exile Bay in 2024

First published by the NSW Bookstall Company in 1915, 1921, 1923

Copyright in this edition © ETT Imprint 2024

ETT IMPRINT
PO Box R1906
Royal Exchange NSW 1225
Australia

ISBN 978-1-923205-12-3 (paper)
ISBN 978-1-923205-48-2 (ebook)

Cover art by Vernon Lorimer
Original drawings by Tom Ferry, and ST Gill.

Designed by Tom Thompson

INTRODUCTION

"A brilliant Australian goldfields tale, in which a murder mystery, thrilling bushranging episodes and fine love story combine to make it one of the most popular of this widely read author's books."

That's what was said of this book a hundred years ago - it gave readers a glimpse of the 1850s, touched on our national love of gold, bushrangers, and with it a secret romance.

Turon Gold was written by a well-read Irishman John Sandes, a journalist, poet and novelist, born on 26 February 1863 at Cork, Ireland. He was educated at Trinity College and got his Bachelor Arts at Magdelene College Oxford, before arriving in Melbourne in 1887, where he worked for the Melbourne *Argus*. In 1903 he took up a position for the *Daily Telegraph* in Sydney where he wrote articles on the gold rushes, bushranging and sporting life, and wrote ten adventure romances. Six were under the pseudonym of Don Delaney.

His first Don Delany book *Gentleman Jack, Bushranger* (1911), followed by *A Rebel Of The Bush* (1913), *Captain of the Gang* (1914) *For Turon Gold: A Tale Of The Fifties* (1915), *The White Champion: The Australian Ring* (1917) and finally *The Escort* (1925)

Sandes was a journalist of some standing in the industry, being the *Daily Telegraph*'s London correspondent from 1919 to his return to Australia in 1922.

To find the background of life at Sofala, Sandes met and corresponded with boxer Larry Foley, who was born in Sofala on the Turon in 1849. Foley became Middleweight Champion of the World in 1879, and taught many of the world's boxing greats including Tommy Burns, and Bob Fitzsimmons. Foley was known as the Captain of the Push, and opened a boxing academy at his White Horse Hotel in George Street Sydney, even fighting two exhibition matches with Jack Johnson in 1907, before he died in Sydney in 1917. *The Captain of the Gang* (1914) and *The White Champion: The Australian Ring* (1917), are direct links with his appreciation and knowledge of Foley's life, as is this book.

Sandes also met the Pryke Brothers, Dan and Frank, both born in Sofala in the 1860s. Their father, John Pryke, opened a hardware store for miners in Sofala in 1851, and took his sons regularly to the Hill End and Tambaroora gold fields. The Pryke brothers had successfully found gold in Australia and New Guinea as early as 1896, and were later feted by Ion Idriess in his *Gold-Dust and Ashes* (1935).

As a journalist he had access to the *Bathurst Free Post* which gave him several story lines for this book, including this one from 'The Turon', December 1853: *Jemmy D'Arcy or Count D'Arcy who escaped from the mounted patrol whilst being conveyed to Bathurst on a charge of murder, was apprehended here a few days ago. He made a desperate attempt to escape from custody, leaping with his handcuffs over the perpendicular precipice near Lucky Point into the river with astonishing alacrity— a height I should suppose of 50 to 60 feet at least. He was captured, however, after receiving sundry cuts and bruises, and was duly forwarded to the brick quadrangle in the centre of your town.*

The main street of Sofala in the early 1850s was over ten kilometres long, and one of Pryke's neighbours were the Delaneys. As the name Don Delaney was known and highly regarded in the area during the 1850s and 60s, Sandes decided on this *nome de plume* for his Australian romantic tales. While organised gangs of bushrangers did not exist on the Turon in the 1850s, many of the future bushrangers earned a living on the fields at that time, and even came back to clean up in the 1860s – Frank Gardiner and Ben Hall had several robberies in Sofala in 1863.

In *For Turon Gold* Esther's decision to adopt male clothing and engage with a bushranging gang, presages Eve Langley's *The Pea Pickers* (1942) where the narrator adopts a male persona – Steve Hart of the Kelly Gang – and men's clothing for itinerant work in the bush.

Sandes however knew of Rosa Praed's *Fugitive Anne: A Romance of the Unexplored Bush* (1902) wherein an married woman fakes her death and travels in disguise through inner Australia with an Aboriginal companion. So here we go, back in time, to the rough and ready world of the 1850s; of bushrangers chased by black-trackers, with characters rugged, intelligent, brave and intrepid.

Tom Thompson

CONTENTS

Dunphy's appearance was so menacing that the good Bishop immediately uplifted his two white podgy little hands.

1

In the Turon Gorge

IF it had not been for Pietro Morosini, their black-browed neighbor, Old Pennycuick's party would have been perfectly satisfied with their claim of 18ft. frontage to the Turon River. They were getting good gold, and Malachi Pennycuick's eyes glistened as he saw the bulge in the leathern bag increasing day by day, and felt the bag growing heavier. Presently he would take it across to the Commissioner's tent, and entrust it to the Commissioner, taking the Government's receipt for it, and it would be sent down by the gold escort to Sydney to be added to the solid nest-egg that old Malachi and his. party had already accumulated.

But Pietro Morosini was a most disagreeable neighbor.

He annoyed old Pennycuick by hovering perpetually round his claim, obviously with the intention of "jumping" it if by any mischance it should be left unoccupied for a moment.

He annoyed David Venn, the young New South Wales native, whom old Pennycuick had taken into the party because of his handiness and resourcefulness, by glaring at him on all occasions with a most unaccountable animosity.

He annoyed young Jack Pennycuick by staring at him with a bold and insolent leer that caused the hot flush of indignation to mantle in Jack's cheeks, because it seemed to say so plainly, "I have seen through your disguise, and I know that you are not what you seem to be."

Last of all, he annoyed Martin Burke, who supplied old Pennycuick with a large percentage of the muscular power required for the profitable working of the claim, and who lived in a gunyah at the back of Pennycuick's tent. Morosini exasperated this honest digger by prowling round the tent at night, plainly for no good purpose. In fact, on the night before this chronicle opens, Martin Burke had loudly threatened that he would split the Italian's ugly mug with an axe next time he found him encroaching on the Pennycuiok tent-space.

By the end of July there were a couple of thousand diggers on the Turon, and all day long the interminable rattle of the cradles resounded as the miners put the dirt through hopper and slide first before carefully panning it off in the tin dish. The whole of the river bank on both sides was taken up as far as the eye could reach, and new arrivals approaching by the coach road from Bathurst could see, when they climbed the last ridge and looked down into the Turon valley, row upon row of tents pitched close together like the encampment of an army.

Pennycuick's claim was at Golden Point, where he had been granted the regulation 18ft. frontage which was allowed for a party of four. It was there that he rocked the cradle and watched the gradual accumulation of the rich residual, while Martin Burke dug down gradually into the bowels of the earth, and David Venn carried the stuff to the cradle, emptying it upon the sieve of the hopper, and Jack Pennycuick poured water from the creek upon the dissolving mass. They were doing well. Occasionally they made as much as three or four ounces in a day.

But Morosini, who, with his mate, Giuseppe Bini, had 9ft. frontage just above old Pennycuicks' claim, could get hardly any return for his labor. A few miserable pennyweights a day was all that the two men usually secured - and often they did not get even that.

The malevolence of the black-browed Pietro increased.

He muttered to Bini that in his opinion old Pennycuick possessed the evil eye. Bini nodded his head gravely, and took to spitting on the ground ostentatiously whenever he passed Malachi.

The Pennycuick party did their best to ignore their unpleasant neighbors. The old Cornish miner, who had a vein of dour religion running through him like a core of ironstone under granite, was accustomed to place a pair of horn spectacles over his pose every evening in the tent and read a chapter of the Word for guidance. He preferred the Old Testament to the New, and his voice swelled with pride as he foretold the fate of all those who declined to walk in the paths of righteousness. One night David and "Jack" had much to say to each other which it was not necessary for old Pennycuick to hear. They sat in the entrance of the large, roomy tent, while Malachi sat at the table, lit by a candle, in the background.

Outside the camp fires blazed high on the banks of the river, and back towards the steep ranges that closed in to make the Turon gorge. The notes of a concertina came faintly through the night air, and a man's voice far away was heard singing "Annie Laurie."

"Her brow was like the snowdrift,
Her neck was like the swan,
Her face it was the fairest
That e'er the sun shone on,
That e'er the sun shone on,
And she's all the world to me,
And for bonnie Annie Laurie,
I'd lay me down an' dee."

"David," said Jack suddenly,"Do you ever think any the worse of me for forgetting that my name is Esther and dressing like a boy so that I can stay with my father and take care of him? "

"I do not think the worse of you, but the better, little girl," said David, pressing the small brown hand that lay in his own.

"And will you always have me for your Annie Laurie? "

"Yes, Esther dear, I will, for indeed, indeed, you're all the world to me."

"And that means that you would do anything at all tor me, doesn't it, David?" whispered Esther Pennycuick contentedly, as she felt David's arm stealing protectingly round her waist.

And David for answer sang under his breath, in a voice that thrilled her :- "And for bonnie Annie Laurie o I'd lay me down an' dee."

"I would not be at that man's mercy for all the gold in
"FOR BONNIE ANNIE LAURIE."

2

"For Bonnie Annie Laurie"

AFTER breakfast next morning, and being furthermore refreshed by a chapter of Isaiah old Malachi, Pennycuick made his way to his claim, muttering to himself: "Their land also is full of silver and gold, neither is there any end of their treasures; their land also is full of horses, neither is there any end to their chariots." But when he reached the claim and looked into the hole he caught his breath with amazement, for Morosini was already in it, and was breaking out the rich washdirt with his pick, while Bini glared forbiddingly, bucket in hand, from the other side.

"Get out of this," snarled old Pennycuick, grasping his spade, "or of a surety I will hew ye in pieces before the Lord."

"No dam fear-a," retorted Pietro. "Dis my claim now. You no work 'ere for t're days."

Malachi was thunderstruck at such mendacity. By the rule of the diggings, if a claim was left unworked for three clear days anyone might take possession of it. But the question did not arise in this case. He had worked at the claim himself on the previous evening. He paused just long enough to remark that the mouths of the heathen were full or cursing and lies and that their feet were swift to shed blood. Then he jumped into the claim, and the sounds of a fierce combat rose from that hole in the ground, and fell on the ears of Trooper Mitford, who was riding slowly along the river bank, not without expectation of some such disturbance.

When Trooper Mitford produced his carbine, and ordered the two combatants to come out of the hole, they obeyed him sulkily, and an adjournment was then made to the Commissioner's tent. Commissioner Grey heard the evidence, i nstantly decided that Morosini was the most fluent liar that he had heard for quite a week, and found in favor of old Pennycuick.

"And now you, Morosini," continued the Commissioner, "just remember that this is a law-abiding field, and as long as I am here it is going to remain so. The next time I find you trying on a game like this I will expel you from the Turon altogether."

Morosini was led out of the Commissioner's tent, muttering angrily, and old Pennycuick made his way back to the river, remarking to himself that the baffled claim-jumper was like unto the men of Gomorrah, and that all they who rebelled should be devoured with the sword, but that Zion was redeemed with judgment, and her convert with righteousness.

When David heard of the trouble he looked grave, and Esther Pennycuick, very slim and boyish in her blue shirt and moleskins, glanced up at the young man anxiously, "Dear," she said, laying her hand on David's sleeve, "try to keep out of that man's way as much as possible. I am sure he means to do us some harm. I can feel it whenever he comes near me."

Of course David comforted her, but the old man's daughter was plainly ill at ease. "I can tell by the way he looks at me that he knows I am a girl, in spite of my boy's clothes," whispered Esther Pennycuick, with a blush. "See, he is looking at us now."

And, sure enough, the ill-omened visage of Pietro scowled at them for a few seconds as he descended into his disappointing claim. David intercepted a hungry look in the Italian's shameless, fierce, dark eyes, as they rested for a moment on the lithe figure in boy's clothes that stood beside him. And then he met an unmistakable glance of hate when he himself encountered the gaze of the unsuccessful digger.

"I wish to heaven that the Commissioner had dealt promptly with the fellow," said David, "for I'm certain that Morosini would be equal to any villainy. And mind you don't stir a step away from the tent, Esther, without me, whatever you do."

The girl looked across to the Italian's claim, and shivered.

"You may be perfectly certain that I will take good care," she said. "I would not be at that man's mercy for all the gold in the Turon."

It was after dinner that Malachi found the nugget. It was a real beauty, of just twelve ounces. It came in one of the loads of stuff that Martin Burke had broken down, and old Pennycuick picked it out of the fissure in the clay-slate, where it lay, with the blade of his knife. Eager was the interest of David and Esther in the find, and loud were their jubilations as they examined it.

Morosini, who had been digging all day, and had scarcely got a "color," heard the exclamations of delight, and quickly realised what had happened. He ground his teeth in rage, and spat furiously on the earth, as also did Bini when the accursed old Englishman with the evil eye knocked off work for the night, and strode off with his three partners, and with nearly £70 worth of gold as the day's product of the claim, from which he (Morosini) had been -in his opinion- so unrighteously dispossessed. It was enough to make a good Calabrian mistrust the ability of his patron saint.

As Pennycuick and his party made their way from the claim to their tent, which was pitched half a mile away on the higher ground, the usual desultory fusillade that was fired soon after sunset fell upon their ears. The diggers were in the habit of firing off their shot-guns, and then ostentatiously reloading the weapons as a warning to any prowlers who might be contemplating an exploit in tent-robbing.

"It shall be a sign and a symbol to the heathen," ejaculated old Malachi piously, as David entered the tent, and bringing out the double-barrelled shotgun, discharged both barrels, and then reloaded the gun slowly and deliberately while standing at the entrance.

Esther watched the operation closely. "Don't forget the caps, David," she said, with a smile.

"You seem to know something about guns," said David, looking at the girl curiously.

"I should think she does, too," put in old Malachi with a grin. "She's as good a quail shot as any man in the West Country."

"Gettin ready for somebody, Venn " inquired Dick Pentreath, a genial giant, who was cooking his supper outside the next tent.

"Ay," said old Malachi, cutting in, "it may be that he shall break the heathen with a rod of iron, and dash them in pieces like a potter's vessel."

"Well, you'll have to be careful, Venn," replied the digger, whe was busy with a beef-steak that he was broiling. The light from the fire showed up his bearded face in the ruddy glow, and David remembered the warning, and the face of the man whe uttered it, long afterwards.

"Commissioner Grey don't like a man to be too quick with his gun," continued the digger. "He was telling the boys this afternoon that it's murder to shoot an unarmed man on account of a suspicion that he might be thinkin' of robbin' you. The Commissioner says he won't have any of them Californian ways on the Turon, an' he has given the boys fair warnin' that the man who shoots another man dead, except in self defence, will go up for murder sure enough."

"Fear not for us, friend, but fear rather for thyself," retorted old Pennycuick sagely, "for though the wicked lie in wait for blood, they shall be overthrown, and the house of the righteous shall stand."

"Oh, all right. Have it your own way, old chap, whatever it is, but don't say I didn't tell you what the Commissioner said. about miscellaneous shooting." The digger finished cooking his steak, and retired into his tent to eat it.

As Esther Pennycuick came out to prepare the evening meal for the party, the scene in the lonely mountain gorge was a strange one. Innumerable watch-fires glowed and gleamed where a few weeks previously the earth was dark and cold-wrapped in a solitude that was almost primeval, for it had been seldom broken in upon except by some blackboy tending the white man's wandering stock.

The girl who had put on boy's dress and ventured so far from civilisation in order to be with her crotchety old father, to whom she was passionately devoted, was almost the only white woman among a crowd of more than two thousand men. The storekeeper's wife and the butcher's wife had gone out to the field, it is true, with their husbands, and there were a few women to be found engaged in domestic work at the two flourishing public houses that speedily sprang into existence on the outskirts of the settlement. But Esther Pennycuick had nothing to say to any of them. Her youth and tenderness, her ardor and chivalrous devotion to those whom she loved, had nothing in common with the stolid qualities of the few white women who foregathered and gossiped and quarrelled on the fringe of the great mass of the gold diggers.

As she stood beside old Pennycuick's tent broiling the meat for the evening meal in the corner of a mighty fire of logs that was used in common by the occupants of all the adjoining tents, the girl looked out upon a canvas city that had grown like a magic realm conjured up by some wizard on the banks of this river, which flowed over sands of gold.

And she was the only girl there!

Great bearded men, with their trousers tucked into high boots, and their rough clothes stained with the many-colored clay, passed and repassed in front of the multitudinous fires, for the nights in July are bitterly cold in the mountains beyond - Bathurst. White tents were interspersed with gunyahs and mia-mias hastily constructed of green branches to form some shelter from the cold, and there were even a few weatherboard structures covered with calico.

Near Golden Point the tents clustered most thickly.

The girl could see the point jutting out boldly, and the dark and winding line that marked the course of the Turon as it flowed down the valley on its way to join the distant Macquarie. She strained her eyes to pierce the gloom out of which this wonderful golden river flowed-this river which had attracted those thousands of men, who were being augmented every day by new arrivals, and among whom were included Pietro Morosini.

Esther Pennycuick shuddered again as she thought of that swarthy Calabrian who had penetrated her disguise. He came from a country where passion was volcanic, and she had caught a look in his eyes that made her afraid.

Her solitude of sex, her immense isolation as a feminine unit in the midst of this vast and restless aggregation of masculine units, was borne in upon her with terrifying force as she gazed upwards at the dark, vague outlines of the mountains that hemmed the narrow valley in on either side, and then at those innumerable fires scattered among the white tents, and throwing their glow upon the bearded face of the diggers who had been drawn into the wilderness by the magnet of the gold.

Happily the task of the moment called back her thoughts and deadened her wandering fears. The beef had to be broiled, and Esther Pennycuiek was able to broil it well. She set out the simple meal appetisingly, and, forgetting all her gloomy apprehensions, she laughed and chatted gaily while she served old Malachi and David Venn and Martin Burke with juicy meat, damper baked in the embers, and great pannikins of tea.

And after the meal, when the men had lighted their pipes, Esther Pennycuick, still in her blue shirt and moleskins, sat on a big log near the fire, between old Malachi and David Venn, the two people that she loved best in the world, and held a hand of each. Martin Burke, who worshipped her privately, and was sworn to secrecy on the subject of her sex, sat afar off, and stared into the fire, wishing that he was twenty again instead of sixty.

From the different fires watch came songs in all the languages of Europe; songs of love, songs of home and little folk-songs, with haunting melodies that began with a trumpet call and ended with a sob.

One of these songs was sung by their friend, Ivan the Russian - an exquisitely tender little air, in a minor key, with queer Slavonic intervals, that caught the very heart strings of the listeners. Ivan, far from home, sang a folk-song of the Volga peasants, beginning thus :-

Stahit gora visokaya, Stahit gora vcsenni hai,

When Jack Pennycuick asked him to come over and explain it, the good-natured Ivan obeyed readily. "Dis song," he said, "it says dat de leaves of de trees dey do fall into de Volga, and de river carries dem away to de sea. In spring-time sall come some more leaves on de trees, but de peasant of de Volga, when he is departed from his 'orne sall see de leaves of springtime on de Volga no more. He is whirled away like de leaf, and so - dat is all."

Esther suddenly felt chilly in spite of the fire, but Ivan was quite cheerful. He produced a bottle of square gin for the entertainment of himself and his friends, and he spoke enthusiastically of the many good qualities of his partners, two young Scotsmen. He went in quest of one of them who could sing. And behold! it was the same young man who had sung "Affine Laurie" on the previous evening.

He sang it again, at the earnest request of Jack Pennycuiok, who seemed to be a particularly nice boy, and also for David Venn.

LICENCES ISSUED—GOLD FOUND AT THE TURON.

ISSUING LICENCES.

3

The Wages of Sin

GRADUALLY the fires were allowed to die down. At last I van the Russian drained the last drop from the bottle of "square face," and lurched off to his camp, followed by the two young Scotsmen.

Esther retired into the tent, and lay down fully dressed on her mattress, as was the custom of the diggers. Old Malachi went next, muttering to himself, "Thou shalt lay up gold as dust, and the gold of Ophir as the stones of the brooks," He placed the heavy leathern bag under his pillow, and the big nugget 'wrapped in a handkerchief beside it.

Last of all David Venn entered the tent, carrying the double-barrelled gun that. he had loaded. He rested the stock on the ground, with the barrels leaning against the tent pole. The gun was equidistant from each of the three occupants of the tent.

Old Malachi blew out the candle.

But none of the three could go to sleep-tired as they all were.

When Esther Pennycuick closed her eyes, she trembled with unreasoning panic, for she seemed to see the dark malevolent face of Morosini, and his hungry eye sthat pierce her disguise and made her shiver with shame and dread.

Old Malachi tossed and turned on his mattress uneasily.

At intervals he felt for the leathern bag full of gold dust, and the big nugget that was wrapped in the handkerchief. He clenched his teeth as he thought of the audacious foreigner, who had tried to jump his claim and rob him of his gold.

David Venn was restless, too. He could not forget the glare of jealous hatred that he had seen in the Italian's eyes. Was it possible, he kept asking himself, that the Dago was plotting mischief?

Even old Martin Burke, in his mia-mia of bushes half a dozen yards away from the tent, was most unusually wakeful. He could not get it out of his head that the black-brewed Italian was "a thafe of the worruld, begob."

The crescent of the moon rose over the ranges and threw a fitful light upon the sleeping camp. Far away a dingo howled.

Morosini moved restlessly on the bags filled with dirty straw that served him for a bed. His tent-mate, Bini, was snoring heavily, overcome by deep potations of "square face." Morosini sat up and listened. The sleeping camp was wrapped in silence. From far away in the mountains came another long, weird, melancholy howl, where some prowling dill-go sought his prey. Morosini felt a thrill of kinship with the prowler.

The Italian's lips were dry and parched. His hungry dark eyes were shining like a cat's. He wanted something - he hardly knew what. First he thought of "Jack" Pennycuick, that lissom girl, whose boy's attire did not deceive him for a moment. She was the only girl on the diggings. Pietro Morosini half rose from his bags of straw, and then fell back again with a snarl. There was her old father, Malachi, an infidel, a heretic, who had assaulted him, Morosini, with a long-handled shovel, and had exposed him to the censure of the Commissioner, Lastly, there was David Venn, who, as anybody with eyes in his head could see, was desperately in love with old Malachi's daughter. But Venn should not have her. No, Corpo di Baccho, he, Morosini, would take care of that. Moreover, there was gold in the tent - much gold - enough gold to enable the possessor of it to obtain all that his heart desired. Thus Morosini communed with himself, until at last he could bear the inaction no longer. He would go forth to the tent of the Pennycuicks. That tent contained a woman. It also contained an enemy, who had struck him blows, and a young rival who was trying to steal the woman from him. Moreover, there was a hoard of gold in the tent.

The wild Calabrian blood was by this time quite beyond control. The thought of the woman, the gold and the opportunity of taking vengeance, all lying ready to hand in the tent that was scarcely a hundred paces distant, completely possessed Morosini. He started up from the bags of straw. He felt for his big sheath-knife, and placed it in his teeth. Then without waking Bini, he crawled out of the tent, and as he did so the wild dog far away in the untrodden solitude called to him once more, with the weird howl that seemed to welcome him as one of the pack.

On his hands and knees, like some four-footed beast of prey, Morosini crawled over the ground with his sheath-knife between his teeth, towards the tent of the Pennycuicks. When he had traversed half the distance, noting that all was silent, he rose to his feet, and put the knife in his pocket.

"Hulloa, Morosini; what's up?"

The Italian looked round with a startled glance, and saw Dick Pentreath, the gigantic Cornishman, sitting in the entrance of his tent, smoking his pipe. "Vot you doin' dere?" asked Pietro, suspiciously.

"Couldn't sleep, my son," said Dick, "so I thought I might as well get up and have a smoke. But wot are you doin' yourself?" And promptly, with true Southern imaginativeness, Pietro Morosini wove his plausible tale.· He was afraid to stay in his tent, because David Venn, the young man who was the mate of the old digger with the evil eye, had threatened to shoot him. The young man was enraged with him, because of his attempt to assert his rights by taking possession of the claim which the old man had abandoned. The young man had sworn to kill him on sight. And, therefore, he, Morosini, dared not stay in his tent. He was on his way, in fact, to ask Dick Pentreath to protect him.

The slow-witted Cornishman listened with astonishment, and ended by fully believing the story.

"True enough. I seen young Venn loading his gun just after sundown," he remarked," an' if you'll take my advice, you'll just keep out of his way till he has cooled down a bit. Ye can coom in 'ere and stay wi' me, if ye're frightened, Pietro, an' I'll 'ave a talk with David in the morning."

But Morosini would not think of accepting the hospitable offer. Body of Bacchus, no. He would just walk about till sunrise, and as soon as the camp was awake he would lay a formal complaint before the Gold Commissioner. So, bidding Dick Pentreath good-night, he disappeared among the lines of tents, and the Cornishman, having finished his pipe, went back to try and get a few hours of sleep before daybreak.

For fully half an hour Morosini waited, trying to frame some coherent plan of action. His pulses were throbbing furiously, and the veins stood out on his forehead, as with his knife in his teeth once more he crept on hands and knees towards the tent of the Pennycuicks. The blood-lust nerved his muscles. The woman-hunger blazed in his eyes. He scarcely knew what he was doing. As he crawled towards the tent, he came upon a large round stone, of several pounds weight, lying half-embedded in the ground. Instinctively his fingers closed over it, and, as he lifted the stone, and felt its weight, the plan, a wild and desperate one, truly, came to him. He was merely a beast of the forest by this time, with only one thought - to seize and get away with his prey.

Creeping to the tent, he realised that the job must be done without noise.

He would stun the two men rapidly, one after the other, by a couple of heavy blows with the stone. Then he would gag the girl and carry her away into the bush.

This was the thought that formulated itself in the brain of Pietro Morosini, while his intended victims tossed in uneasy slumbers on the mattresses stuffed with straw. With the knife in his teeth, and the heavy stone in his hand, he crept over the rough ground, the embodiment of brutal malignity, and yet as elusive as a shadow. Thus the tiger stalks his victim in the jungle.

When he reached the tent Pietro tried the "fly," and found it securely fastened. He could hear the heavy breathing of the sleepers inside.

Esther Pennycuick dreamed restlessly as she lay fully dressed in Crimean shirt and moleskin trousers under her heavy sheepskin rug. She dreamed that she was walking hand in hand with David through a great plain, strewn with - wild flowers. The sun was shirring, and there were blue hills in the distance. They had crossed a creek, and were approaching a great boulder of basalt. As they passed the boulder, she happened to look round over her shoulder. She saw a huge black snake which had which had wriggled from under a corner of the boulder, lift its head, and its cruel, glassy eyes held her fascinated. She realised that it was about to strike - at David.

With her heart bounding furiously from sheer fright, the girl awoke. She was fully awake on the instant. The interior of the tent was not dark. A big hole near the top let in a few misty beams of moonlight. The tent was old and worn. There were several holes in it.

Her eyes fell first on the gun leaning against the tent-pole, and then on the motionless forms of her father and David Venn. Were they asleep? She could not tell.

Lifting her eyes to the side of the tent, she saw that the moonlight which had been entering through a small hole near the "fly" of the tent suddenly obscured. Something was blocking up the hole. To her horror she saw two eyes looking at her through the hole in the tent - two eyes that made her think at once of the cruel, glassy eyes of the black snake in her dream. Paralysed with fear, she continued to gaze at those eyes.

The heavy breathing of one of the sleepers - she could not be sure which stopped at that moment. Ha! This was terrible. She must act - act - act !

There was a quick cry, and then a flash, and a loud report. The tent was full of smoke.

One of the three occupants of the tent had seized the gun and fired point blank through the canvas at the head outside.

The face of the man who had been looking into the tent with those cruel, glassy, snakelike eyes of his, was all shot to pieces. And the body, after a few convulsive wriggles, lay motionless on the cold earth, under the misty beams of the moon.

Next moment the fly of the tent was torn open, and as Dick Pentreath emerged from his own tent close by, he saw David Venn with the smoking gun still in his hand, looking down on the dead man.

A score or more of miners had poured from their tents at the report of the gun, and, seeing them, David Venn, with the weapon still in his hand, started to run.

He reached the river, with the miners in full cry close behind him. Dashing into the stream, he waded across and emerged on the opposite bank. In the darkness and confusion they lost sight of him, and remembering that one barrel of his gun was stilt loaded, they did not press home the chase, preferring to wait until daylight.

When Trooper Mitford, closely followed by Mr. Commissioner Grey, arrived on-the scene, they found a dead man, with his features blown to pieces beyond all possibility of recognition, lying outside the Pennycuick's tent.

The youth Jack Pennycuick, was as pale as death, and seemed to have been struck dumb by the tragedy. But old Malachi confronted the representatives of the law with glaring eyes, and mumbled texts with extraordinary volubility.

"What is the crazy old fool talking about ~" exclaimed the Commissioner testily, as Malachi continued to pour out incoherent denunciations. "David Venn is our man, Mitford."

"Yes, sir," assented the well-disciplined trooper. "Indeed he is, sir."

"And, by heaven, if he murdered this poor devil of a Dago in cold blood, he shall swing for it," snapped the Commissioner. "Take it couple of black trackers with you at daylight, Mitford, and see that you bring him back, alive or dead, before mid-day."

The trooper saluted, and moved off to catch his horse, while Esther Pennycuick, sitting on a big log near the tent, covered her face with her hands and prayed.

4

What the Trooper Saw

COMMISSIONER GREY held an informal inquiry at the Government tent in the forenoon. Giuseppe Bini became almost incoherent in his volubility as he identified the dead man. Yes, it was the body of Pietro Morosini, his mate. He, Bini, had been aware from the first that a calamity would fall upon his mate. He first experienced that feeling when he noticed that "il vecchio" had the evil eye.

The Commissioner was puzzled. "Who was 'il vecchio,' 'the old man' ~"

Bini pointed towards Malachi Pennycuick, keeping his own gaze rigorously averted from the old Cornishman. Then he spat on the ground ostentatiously.

"Shure, he can't shpake the quare name of him, bein' only a Dago, yer 'anner," interpolated Constable Mahoney, in an audible aside.

But Bini declined even to attempt to pronounce the hated and dreaded name. He crossed his fingers nervously whenever he became conscious that old Malachi had his eye on him, and he proceeded to relate with great particularity a wholly imaginary conversation between himself and Morosini on the previous day. Morosini had told him that David Venn had threatened to shoot the pair of them on sight, and he, Bini, consequently went so much in fear of his life that he had been compelled to arm himself. Whereupon he drew a long, thin, straight-bladed knife out of his boot, and Constable Mahoney immediately confiscated it, remarking at the same time: "It'll be safer wid me, me son."

The next witness was Dick Pentreath, whe stood up in front of the plain, deal table at which the Commissioner sat, and related his nocturnal interview with Morosini. The man was wandering about the camp in evident fear of his life, dreading to remain in his own tent. He had distinctly stated that David Venn had threatened to shoot him. It was about half an hour after retiring into his own tent that he, witness, had heard the report of a gun. Running out of his tent, he saw David Venn with a gun in his hand, looking down on the dead man, The barrel of the gun was still smoking.

The Commissioner had been taking a note of the evidence in a book. He closed his note-beck with a snap. "I do not think I need go any further at this stage," he said. "You will keep the old man, Pennycuick, and his son, under observation, Mahoney. They may be wanted to give evidence at the trial of the man Venn. He will be formally charged with murder. A more cruel, cold-blooded and cowardly murder I have never heard of. The inquiry is adjourned."

Among the miners who streamed out of the Government tent was Malachi Pennycuick, with Esther - her sex still unsuspected - by his side. The girl was very pale. Her close-pressed lips signalled her determination to keep silence.

But Malachi, staring straight in front of him, muttered continually. "Thus saith the prophet Isaiah," he said, turning round to glare at the Government tent, "None calleth for justice, not any pleadeth for truth; they trust in vanity and speak lies; they conceive mischief, and bring forth iniquity. Their feet run to evil, and they make haste to shed innocent blood; their thoughts are thoughts of iniquity; wasting and destruction are in their paths. Therefore is judgment far from us, neither doth justice overtake us."

But nobody paid any attention to his obscure utterances.

All were too much intent upon their immediate quest for gold, which was more important for them than even the avenging of blood.

Meanwhile Trooper Mitford and his black satellites, Jimmy and Jacky, had a long, stern chase on the trail of David Venn. Mitford was mounted, but the blacks trav¬elled afoot. Not until the morning of the fifth day after leaving the Turon did they return, bringing in their prisoner handcuffed to the trooper's stirrup.

Captors and captive alike were worn out, and Mr. Commissioner Grey looked with astonishment at the gaunt face and tattered rags of Mitford, and at the limping horse by whose side marched a prisoner whose bleeding feet protruded through the remains of his used-up boots, and whose bloodshot eyes roved eagerly around as though in search of somebody whose presence he desired intensely. Even Jimmy and Jacky threw themselves on the ground with unmistakable grunts of relief. They were a pair of very tired black trackers.

"Good heavens! Mitford, where have you been?" inquired the amazed Commissioner.

The trooper, grim and hollow-cheeked, saluted, "We tracked him over the ranges," he said, "right away to the Macquarie River - a good eighty miles from here by the roundabout line he took. We followed his tracks up the bank of the river. I pushed across to Ponto Island, in the middle of the Macquarie, and found his camp. He was worn out with travelling, and when I got to him at last he was asleep. I secured his gun, and he only awoke as I slipped the handcuffs on him. He had no chance to put up a fight, and there was nothing for it but to come along quietly. So there he is."

"David Venn," said the Commissioner, eyeing the prisoner, whe looked more like a scarecrow than a man, "I shall resume the adjourned inquiry into the death of Pietro Morosini at ten o'clock to-morrow morning. You will then have an opportunity of presenting any defence that you can offer. In the event of a 'prima facie' case being made out against you to my satisfaction, you will be sent to Bathurst to take your trial on a charge of murder. Trooper Mitford, remove your prisoner."

The Commissioner lit a cigar, and Mitford motioned to the prisoner to accompany him to the police tent, where the constables were camped who kept order in the great assemblage of miners gathered on the banks of the Turon.

Davin Venn followed Mitford quietly, and took the food and drink that the constables set before him out of their own rations. He was ravenously hungry, and as he ate the mutton and damper and drank the big pannikin of tea in silence, he heard Trooper Mitford recounting to Trooper Mahoney all the incidents of the long chase. At times Mitford would interrupt his narrative to question the prisoner as to his line of flight.

Mitford sat at one side of the table, resting an elbow on it and emphasising the points of his tale with his lifted forefinger. Mahoney sat on the other side with his cap on the ground beside him, and David Venn sat at the end on an upturned candlebox, since there were only two chairs in the tent. The Government provided no shelter or luxuries for its prisoners, who were dealt with in a very primitive fashion, as will presently appear.

"So we camped on the first night at the foot of Bald Hill," said Mitford, continuing his narrative. "I guessed that he would make for the Macquarie, and, as the night was very cold, I had an idea that he might light a fire, not thinking that we would be so hot on his tracks."

"Um!" grunted Mahoney, doubtfully. "Ad' did ye light a fire, me son ~"

"No," said Davin Venn, who was listening with quiet interest to the reasoning of his pursuer.

"Well, anyhow, I thought it was quite likely that he might light one," said Mitford testily, "and I made up my mind to climb up to the top of Bald Hill so that I could see any fire that was lighted in the valley or en the side of the ranges opposite. So, after a short rest and a bit of tucker, I left my old horse with the hobbles on him at the bottom of the mountain, and I took Jimmy and Jacky with me and started up. It was so infernally dark that we had to cut bark torches before we could find a way up the mountain - roughest bit of country I've seen for a long while. Jimmy and Jacky were grumbling all the time. 'White pfeller bin sit down alonga creek,' they said, 'Not sit down alonga mountain.' But I kept 'em at it, an' it was just midnight when we got to the top."

"Nothin' to see, of course," said Mahoney. "Ye might have spared yersilf the trouble."

"Wait a bit," continued Trooper Mitford. "I didn't find the man that I was after, but I found something else that I never expected."

Even David Venn became keenly interested in the trooper's story. With his elbows on the table, and his chin supported on the upturned palms of his hands, he listened to Mitford with close attention.

"I made Jacky climb a big blackbutt on the edge of the plateau looking down into the next valley," said Mitford, " and I told him to keep his eye open for smoke. The moon was nearly full, and I could see the slope of the range opposite as plain as the nose on your face. All of a sudden Jacky lets out a grunt of astonishment, and sings out that there was a 'big pfeller fire' among the rocks at the foot of the range."

David Venn was p'ainly as much surprised as Mahoney at the news. He wondered vaguely who it was that had camped in. that lonely valley on the same night that he struggled through it, making for the Macquarie with hunger gnawing at his stomach, but the light of a great resolve warming his heart.

"The valley behind Bald Hill 'ud be in Montgomery's run, I'm thinkin'," said Mahoney, "but sure it wouldn't carry a sheep to the hundred acres, an' there's not a shep¬herd been near ut for the last twelve munts.'

"That's what I thought," said Mitford, "and that's why I made sure I had my man without further any trouble. I sent Jimmy back for my horse by the way we came, with instructions to bring him round and meet us on the other side of the mountain. Then I made a dash' for it with Jacky, and we scrambled down the side of the range, with the big stones sliding away under our feet and rattling down into the valley, enough to wake the dead. Reckon it took us less than an hour to get to the bottom of the mountain, and there I found Jimmy holding my horse and grinning with excitement. 'See here, boss,' says Jimmy, 'mine bin tinkit soon catchit plenty white pfeller.' He said something to Jacky in hia own lingo, and Jacky started to run across the valley as hard as he could pelt."

"An' what was the mare's nest?" inquired Mahoney, suspiciously, as he pulled at his little black clay pipe.

"No mare's nest at all, my lad," said Mitford, with unruffled serenity. "But the mare was there all right - three of 'em, in fact. They might have been horses for all I know, but they were certainly one or the other, for I saw the hoofmarks in the soft ground distinctly."

David Venn was quite excited now. He was breathing hard, and his eyes were very wide open.

"Jimmy and Jacky were about fifty yards in front of me," said

Trooper Mitford. "They were racing along the newly-made tracks, and all I had to do was to keep 'em in sight."

"An' where did the tracks lead to?" inquired Mahoney, who could no longer conceal his interest in the strange discovery.

"Straight up to the fire, of course," said Mitford. "The fire was burning brightly when we got there. There was a billy full of tea beside it, and some burned damper and mutton on the ground. I found the remains of a newly-killed sheep in the bush about twenty yards from the fire.

The men must have heard us clattering down the side of the mountain, and probably they saw Jimmy, too, and recognised the old bay for a trooper's horse. They couldn't have been gone many minutes before Jacky and I reached the bottom of the mountain."

"How many men were there?" inquired Mahoney, incredulously.

"There were three men, so Jacky told me, after looking at their tracks," said Mitford, "and one of them was lame; or, at any rate, he walked with a decided limp."

"An' who do ye think they were ?" asked Mahoney, half envious of his comrade's adventure, but still half unbelieving.

Trooper Mitford cut himself a pipeful of tobacco from his plug very deliberately, and rolled it in his strong hands.

"Bushrangers," he said.

J.A BLUNDELL &Co

Bushrangers attack a gold escort in the Central West of New South Wales.

5

On the Chain

TROOPER MAHONEY leaped up from his chair and upset it in his excitement.

"Holy Smoke;" said he, "that must have been Jack Dunphy's gang, an' the man with the limp must have been the black-bearded felly that got away with my bullet in him the day we chased 'em up at Carson's place."

He would hardly listen to Mitford's long story of the chase and arrest of David Venn on Ponto Island, and of the hardships and semi-starvation of the return journey.

"The Commissioner was saying to me only the other day that he thought Dunphy was still in the district," he remarked, "and sure, I'd be havin' a thry for him mesilf while the thracks are fresh, only Jimmy and Jacky will be wantin' a day's rest before we take 'em out again. But, annyway, Tom, what'll we be doing with this chap Venn?"

"He'll have to go on the chain," said Mitford, curtly. David Venn flushed a dusky red: He realised the indignity that awaited him, but he made up his mind to suffer it with all the patience that he could muster. He was sustained by a secret consolation, of which the two troopers knew nothing.

"Come along, Venn," said Mitford, as soon as the simple meal was finished. "We've no lock-up here, you know. I'll have to put you on the chain with the others."

Mitford and Mahoney, with their prisoner walking between them, made their way to the outskirts of the encampment. It was now early in the afternoon, and the rocking of the innumerable cradles in which the gold-bearing wash-dirt was being treated filled the whole valley with a peculiar rattling hum, like no other sound in the world.

When they reached the end of the long lines of tents and mia-mias they came in sight of "the chain," the rough and ready device of police. officers who were obliged to keep prisoners in custody, and who had none of the resources of civilisation in the shape of gaols or lock-ups to enable them to perform the duty which that rough society laid upon them of segregating the unfit from the fit.

A strong bullock-chain, about twenty-five yards in length, was firmly bolted at one end to a big gum-tree and at the other end to a convenient stump. Along this chain, and strung to it like pendants on a necklace, were all those offenders against law and order whose presence among the respectable diggers of the encampment could not be tolerated until they had purged themselves of their offences by a suitable period of isolation.

Dangerous criminals were kept on tho chain temporarily, until an opportunity occurred of sending them to Bathurst, where there was a gaol, and where justice could be dispensed with proper formalities. Drunks and brawlers, cardsharpers, gold-stealers, swindlers of all kinds, and men, usually foreigners, who resorted to the knife instead of the fist as a means of settling disputes, were all brought to the chain, and kept there during the hours of daylight, attached by their handcuffs to the stout iron links.

At night the drunks and minor offenders were unchained, and allowed to depart to their own quarters, with a caution and a threat of permanent expulsion from the field unless they mended their ways. But those who were charged with graver crimes, such as murder, attempted murder, or gold-stealing, were taken off the chain early in the night and were accommodated with shelter and covering in the police camp, with a sentry on duty all night to guard against escape.

When David Venn and the two constables arrived at the site of this open-air prison, they found it already tenanted by a varied assortment of offenders. There were six men on the chain altogether,

With the prisoner walking between them,
they made their way to the encampment.

and Mahoney made a brief catalogue of them.

"They won't hurt ye, me son," he said to Venn, "an' sure, ye'll only be here for the day, bekase the Commis¬sioner 'ul sind ye in to Bathurst ter-morrer to the gaol. Thim's two drunks at the ind av the chain. I put 'em here meself to kapo 'em out of harrum. The ould felly next to them is the worst ould thafe in the camp. I wint troo his tint yesterday, an' found enough shtuff to stock a township in ut. Picks an' billies an' blankets an' all. The min have been reportin' the loss of them things for the lasht week an' more. The chap next to him is a Spanish man that drew a knife on me 'cause I cudn't understand him, so I knocked him down wid the heel av me fisht, an' anchored him here to get cool." And then, to the scowling Spaniard: "How are ye feeling now, me son?"

The black-browed little Spaniard glared at his oppressor, and spat on the ground before letting fly a volley of unintelligible remarks at a high rate of velocity.

"Sure, I can't ondersthand him," said Mahoney philosophically, "an' he can't onderstand me ayther, so we've just got to make the best of it."

"Who is the chap next to the Spaniard ~" asked Mitford.

"I belave he's a young Englishman, but I wudn't take me oat' on it," said Mahoney, scratching his head. "bekase I can't ondersthand what he do be sayin' no more than the Spaniard. I found him fighting 'wid a big navvy chap about twice his own weight, an' as he wudn't let up on it, I put me arms around him an' fell on him. Then I brought him here, an' the Commissioner can get an intarpreter in the mornin' to see what it's all about, for I'm sure I can't find out."

The Englishman, after fixing a monocle in his eye, began to explain to Mitford eagerly that he was a university graduate, studying for the Church, but that he had missed the track and landed at Turon instead. He was having a friendly turn-up with a navvy, just to keep his hand in, when this incomprehensible policeman suddenly attacked him and fell on him.

"That's all right," said Mitford, "you can tell your story to the Commissioner in the morning, and I hope for your sake that you'll be able to make him understand it. Who's his mate, Mahoney?" Mitford pointed to a dishevelled individual, who was handcuffed a couple of yards away from the disgusted university graduate, and was hiccupping out: "We won't go home till mor-horning, till daylight doth appear," at the top of a particularly husky voice.

"Faix, I can't rightly say who he is," replied Mahoney, scanning the last man on the chain attentively. "I found him lasht night lyin' on the ground close up to the Commissioner's tent, an' be rason of all the gold in the Guv'ment box, that's waitin' for the escort, I t'ought I'd better have a look at him. But he was that drunk he cudn't say a wurrd. So I just humped him along here to give him time to find his senses again. He's a stranger to me. I never set eyes on him befure." .

"Ask him what his name is?" said Mitford quietly. "Fwat's yer name, mate?" bellowed Mahoney, in the tone that he was accustomed to employ in addressing a deaf man or a foreigner.

"We won't go home till mor-horning, till daylight doth appear," sang the incoherent stranger, dancing up and down so that he agitated the whole length of the chain violently, and drew upon himself black looks and curses from all the handcuffed captives attached to it.

"Oh, let him alone," said Mitford disgustedly. "He won't be right until he has had a night's sleep. Come along, Venn."

David advanced, flushed and shivering with the shame of it all. Yet the zeal of a martyr in a great cause warmed his heart, and an inscrutable smile of happiness played upon his lips as he held out his handcuffed hands to the trooper. Mitford quickly slipped the short connecting chain of the handcuffs through one of the links of the bullock chain, and refastened it.

Before he went away a sudden thought seemed to strike him.

"If you care to make ny statement to me, Venn, about the matter that you are charged with," he said, "it is my duty to hear it. You need not say anything, but if you want to ease your conscience you may do so. I have to warn you that anything you do say will be taken down by me in writing and may be used in evidence against you."

"Not here," said David, looking round hurriedly at the other prisoners on the chain. "Unfasten me for a minute, and let me go a little distance away from here, and I will make a statement to you."

So Trooper Mitford, highly gratified at the additional importance that a confession by the prisoner would confer upon him, unfastened the handcuffs again. Already in imagination he could hear the judge complimenting him upon the skill and intelligence with which he had handled the case.

He took David Venn away to a big stringy-bark that stood at some distance from the bullock chain, and directed him to sit down on the ground. Mahoney came, too, to act as a witness. The two constables sat down, one on each side of their prisoner, and Mitford produced his notebook.

"Now," he said, "fire away."

So David Venn told his story in simple and telling language, down to the point at which he and Pennycuicks had retired for the night into their tent.

"But when Pentreath saw you," said Mitford, "you were looking down upon the dead man who was lying close to the tent, and you held the still smoking gun in your hand."

"That is so," said David.

"And you admit that you shot him?" continued Mahoney.

"Yes," said David slowly, "I admit that I shot him. I did it because I was afraid that he intended to do some injury to me."

"That will do," said Mitford. He read over the statement in his notebook to David, and David signed it. Each of the troopers signed it, also, as witnesses. The three men returned to the stretched bullock-chain and Mitford refastened David Venn's handcuffs to a link a couple of yards away from the shock-headed stranger who was still roaring out in most unmelodious accents his determination not to return to his domicile before daylight.

6

Off the Chain

IT was late in the afternoon when Mitford and Mahoney left David
Venn with a promise that they would return at nine o'clock and conduct
him to the police camp for the night.

They had hardly gone when the shock-headed stranger
miraculously recovered his senses and ceased to outrage the peaceful
valley of the Turon with Bacchanalian song.

"Say, mate," he asked in a husky whisper, "what did they pinch
you for?"

"Murder," said David laconically. He did not want to be
annoyed by this bibulous one. He had to think, and think hard.

"Murder," echoed the stranger, with a shout of surprise.

"By the Lord, you don't seem to think much of it. How did it
happen?"

David briefly recounted the quarrel with Morosini and the tragic
death of the Italian. The stranger was evidently impressed, and surveyed
David with a new respect. Moreover, he was really quite astonishingly
sober. David found himself wondering how the stranger, who gave the
name of Jim Grogan, could have so suddenly emerged from a condition
of crazy insobriety to one of a singular clearness of mind. The man was
not only eager for information, but he appeared to weigh it carefully, and
to form definite conclusions concerning it.

"You were quite drunk ten minutes ago," said David.

"Was I?" said Jim Grogan innocently.

"And you are quite sober now .. How do you account for it?"

"I was not nearly so drunk as I seemed," replied Grogan, placing
his left forefinger along the side of his nose with a gesture indicative of a
remarkable nature of cunning and rascality.

David was still trying to solve the riddle when he heard a soft whistle and then a well-known voice that spoke his name. Looking behind him, he saw "Jack" Pennycuick running eagerly towards him. With her slouched hat, her close cropped hair, a black handkerchief knotted loosely about her neck, a Crimean shirt and moleskins, with high boots all stained with clay, the girl looked just like a handsome boy. She ran up to David panting, but noticing that Jim Grogan was regarding her with an inquisitive stare, she restrained her eagerness and scarcely even glanced at David.

"This is my mate, Jack Pennycuick," said David to Jim Grogan, "and we have a good deal to say to each other."

Jack had brought David a pipe and a plug of tobacco.

Cutting the plug in half, the girl handed Jim Grogan one of the pieces at David's request, and Grogan proceeded to chew it voraciously.

"All right; get on with your yabber-yabber," exclaimed the genial Grogan, "and don't mind me." He turned his back ostentatiously on the pair of them and went on chewing his plug with evident enjoyment.

David and Esther Pennycuick spoke rapidly in subdued tones. The girl was very pale and excited.

"David, dear," she said, "what agonies I have suffered since you went away. And now they have caught you, and you will be sent for trial at Bathurst, and they will take me there, too, to give evidence against you, and David, I can't, I can't, I can't."

"Yes you can," said David firmly, "and if the worst comes to the worst you must. It doesn't matter what they do to me. Your double secret must be kept at all costs-the secret that you are a girl, and the secret that you-you-you took that gun to save your honour, if not your life. Morally I know that you are innocent of that man's blood. But to prove that innocence would be difficult, and it would mean that judge and jury, and all the world would have to be told that you are a girl."

"David! David!" The girl flushed a sudden rosy red, and

then the tide of colour ebbed, leaving her face deadly pale. She seemed to be the prey of an emotion of quite unusual intensity.

"They would think badly of you, dear," said David slowly, "if they found that you were really a girl, and that-that you let me sleep in a corner of your tent."

"Don't, David, don't. I can't bear it."

"It was for that reason principally that I did what I did," said Venn. "If you had been arrested for killing Morosini, you might have escaped, at any rate with a term of imprisonment, but your good name would have, been besmirched. As it is, I shall be able to plead that the man threatened us, and that he was going to steal our gold."

"But he wasn't," said Esther, trembling violently.

"I know that he wasn't," said David very softly, under his breath. "I know what he was coming for. You must not tremble and cry like that, dear. Grogan will see you!"

Esther Pennycuick had to invoke all her will-power and all her power for self restraint. She felt the solid earth slipping from under her feet. Could she let this man, whom she loved with such devotion, and who loved her so passionately, take upon his own shoulders, for her sake, the guilt of a crime which was not his ? Appearances were dead against him. He had arranged all that himself. Could she stand by and let him be taken away to Bathurst to be tried for his life-perhaps even to undergo the last dread penalty of the law-when by a word she might save him? But, oh, at what cost! The alternative that presented itself to Esther Pennycuick's mind was a terrible one. There was no escape from the dilemma apparent to her mind as she searched desperately for a way out. It seemed that she must either send her lover to his doom, or else-. Ah, there was a third course after all. Supposing that David could escape, even at that late hour! Supposing that he could get right away into the solitudes of that unknown bush which terrified her with its mysterious vastness and silence because of her English birth and rearing, but which had no terrors for him, since he was familiar with it from childhood.

"Esther, dear, what are you thinking of?" asked David, for

the girl's lips were moving silently, as though in prayer.

"I was thinking, David, that you might even yet escape," said Esther Pennycuick, "if only I could help you. I was thinking that you might get clear away from this, and -and never come back again. She had raised her voice in the wild excitement of the thought and there was a sob in it as she took in the full meaning of David's escape as far as she was concerned. In any case it seemed that she must lose him, and she almost broke down as the conviction of her loss was bore in upon her.

"Wot's all this about escaping an' gettin' clear away?" It was Grogan's voice that interrupted the murmured conversation. Esther had raised her voice unintentionally and Grogan had been quick to hear it.

"It's only a mad dream," said David bitterly. "My mate, Jack Pennycuick here, was thinking that I might make a successful bolt for it."

"So you might, and easily enough too, if I went with you," said Jim Grogan in low, distinct tones.

David and Esther started and turned towards Grogan as though by a common impulse.

"What do you mean?" asked David breathlessly.

"I'll soon show you, if your mate there will get me a file," replied Grogan. "It'll be dark by seven o'clock, and Mitford and Mahoney won't come back before nine. We'll slip out of the bracelets an' be half way to the ranges before they know we're gone."

"I tried that once already," said David bitterly, "and they hunted me with black-trackers and got me at last when I was asleep."

But Jim Grogan possessed unbounded confidence and displayed an astonishing knowledge of the geography of the district. He pressed David hard, and David, who was really anxious to be persuaded, quickly withdrew all objections.

Esther Pennycuick slipped away to her father's tent and presently returned with a small file.

"Smart boy," said Grogan approvingly, "you ought to come with us."

But David vehemently protested. Jack would have to stay and look after the old man. Besides, there was no reason why Jack should become a fugitive. He added that he himself would work his way back to Sydney and would then write to Jack and arrange for the Pennycuicks to go with him to Victoria and try the diggings at Ballarat.

Jim Grogan merely grunted and set to work with the file, covering his operations from the other prisoners on the chain by turning his back on them and resuming the incoherent drunken ditties that had already deceived both David and the troopers.

In the middle of winter, in that remote mountain valley, it was quite dark by six o'clock. Camp fires were already blazing in front of the miners' tents, and Jim Grogan began to get impatient. With his file he cut through the short length of the handcuff-chain that was passed through one of the links of the bullock chain, and was free. Then he rapidly performed the same office for David.

"Leave the bracelets on your wrists for the present," he muttered. "They won't do any harm, and I'll show you how to get them off later on. Now, then, come along."

The parting between David and Esther Pennycuick was a bitter ordeal, and Jim Grogan cursed violently at the delay.

"Esther, my darling," said David, "I am going away now with Grogan, but I shall meet you again soon. You will come down to Sydney with the old man, and we will slip away to the diggings in Victoria, and there we shall be together again, and all this hideous tragedy will be forgotten for ever."

"David, David," sobbed Esther. "How can I let you go?"

"It is for your sake I am going, dear one," whispered David, "to save you from the disgrace as well as the danger that would come to you if the police knew that it was you who-who--"

"Don't, David, don't," said Esther through her sobs.

"I can't bear it. I can't bear it."

"What the - are you two jawin' about?" exclaimed Grogan angrily. "Anybody 'ud think you were a pair of lovers. Come on, Venn."

So David tore himself away from Esther and followed Grogan, whe made through the darkness towards the river. And as David looked back towards the queer bunch of captives whom he had left, and towards the girl who stood by the bullock-chain looking out into the darkness, he heard from the camp fire far away the voice of the young Scotchman singing -

"And for bonnie Annie Laurie, I'd lay me doon and dee."

But Esther Pennycuick, pale and tearless now, crouched in her boy's dress by that grotesque *alfresco* prison from which two of the captives had just escaped, and prayed with dry sobs: "O, God, forgive me for this that I have done."

7

The Hut in the Ranges

"COME on," said the man who had called himself

Grogan, as he plunged through the Turon at a point where the water was barely above his knees, and dashed over the open ground in the dark at a pace that showed he knew every inch of the ground.

David followed him panting. He rejoiced in the thought that he was free once more, and a thrill of delight came over him as he realised that his second escape helped to fasten the guilt of the homicide irrevocably upon him and to relieve Esther Pennycuick of the danger of being suspected of .it.

The man in front of him was range bred, and he moved with the speed and certainty of a wild animal, been in the most broken country. Half walking and half running, he breasted the first forbidding range that looked down upon the valley and presently struck the coach road to Bathurst, Crossing the road, he plunged again into rocky, lightly timbered country, while David Venn toiled after him at his best pace, in spite of many stumbles.

"Hold on a minute, Grogan," called David, after they had been travelling for a little more than an hour, "I'm all out." He pitched forward and fell heavily. Want of food and the excessive fatigue of his previous journey had exhausted his strength. The man was completely done.

Grogan ran back and picked him up. "We've only half a mile more to go," he said encouragingly, "so you must stick it out. It's Kennedy's hut or Bathurst gaol for us, an' I reckon the hut'll do us all right. Push on if ye don't want to be lagged again, an' maybe scragged as well."

With his heart well nigh bursting, and his legs trembling under him, David struggled on, while Grogan, who seemed incapable of feeling fatigue, held him by the arm in an iron grip that many times saved him from falling.

Ten minutes more of this blind, bewildering stumbling agony brought David and his guide to a rude hut, built on the edge of a grassy plateau.

"Here we are at last," muttered Grogan.

He gave a low whistle. The door of the hut opened cautiously, and a huge head, covered with a shock of red hair, emerged slowly.

"Shure, what's kapin' ye?" said the red-haired man in an eager voice, "I wuz expectin' ye lasht night. Where's the shtuff?"

"Blowed if I know," said Grogan angrily. "At any rate, I haven't got it. Hurry up and get me some rum in a pannikin, for this chap that I've got with me. He's very nearly done."

"Och, millia murther," ejaculated Darby Kennedy, seeing David for the first time. "I t'ought it was Tom Warburton ye had wid yeo An' who might this young felly be at all at all."

"Never mind askin' questions," said Grogan, angrily, stamping his foot. "Get the rum, de ye hear?"

The red-haired man disappeared into the hut, and came back with a pannikin, which he held to David's lips. Revived by the potent liquor, David looked round him with surprise, and saw that the hut stood in a little hollow, almost surrounded by hills. Only towards the north was the ground open. Narrow at the hut, it widened into a valley, covered with coarse herbage, and practicable for horsemen. In the dim starlight, this widening valley trended away into an illimitable distance and David quickly realised that his way of escape passed directly into that vista, which led into the unknown. There was no other way out. He looked inquiringly in the direction of the hut, into which the red-haired man had disappeared, and from which came the appetising smell of broiling mutton.

"Darby Kennedy is a shepherd," said Grogan. "He looks after the sheep on Montgomery's run, and this is a corner of it. We find him very useful occasionally, and there's always a good meal to be got here."

"Supper's ready," bawled Kennedy, and David followed his new friend into the hut with some misgivings. However his apprehensions did not affect his appetite, and he found Darby Kennedy's broiled mutton very much to his liking.

"One advantage of being a shepherd," said Grogan with a grin, "is that you need never be short of mutton."

David was still applying himself to the absent Montgomery's mutton when he was startled by the whinnying of a horse close at hand, and leaped to his feet with the unchewed lump between his teeth. "What's that?" he cried sharply, expecting every moment to hear the clank of the trooper's spurs and the voice of the pursuer summoning him back to custody.

Grogan laughed. "I left my horse in Darby's care," he said, "when I went down on a little bit of business to Golden Point. I wasn't able to transact the business, owing to Trooper Mahoney's interference, but, thanks to that little file that your mate brought us, I have got back safe and sound. That was my horse you heard outside."

"The brown horse is wid him, too," interrupted Darby. "I brought a friend of mine, Tom Warburton, with me," said the man who had called himself Grogan, "and he left his horse here, too. He went down to Golden Point with me, but he was luckier than I was. He must be there still, so you can have his horse."

"But who are you, then?" enquired David Venn, with a vague premonition that fate or chance, he knew not which, had taken charge of his future when he was handcuffed to the bullock-chain next to this sinewy Hercules.

"I'm Jack Dunphy," said the man who had called himself Grogan.

In one swift instant David realised that, in sacrificing himself to save Esther Pennycuick, he had mortgaged his liberty of action irrevocably. He had escaped from custody in order to safeguard her secret, but the accident of circumstances had thrown him into the companionship of the notorious Dunphy, and there was no escape from that companionship. Without the assistance of Dunphy he would be recaptured by the police and the black-trackers as certainly as he had been taken by them on Ponto Island. But with Dunphy's aid he could probably elude pursuit indefinitely. The strange logic of events had decreed that for Esther's sake - for the sake of her liberty and her good name - he must ally himself with this leader of a desperate gang of men.. with whose exploits the whole colony was beginning to ring.

David Venn accepted the inevitable.

"Well, young fellow," said Dunphy, with a half humorous twinkle in his eye, "arc you going off by yourself on foot to be caught again by Mitford and the blackfellows, or are you coming with me on the spare horse that is hobbled behind the hut?"

"I'm coming with you," said David Venn, resolutely.

To save the honor and the life of the woman he loved, he would take definitely to the bush, he would face the dangers, the hardships, the constant anxieties, and, possibly, the shameful death that awaited most of those who pitted themselves and their strength against the best intelligence and unlimited power of organised society.

Dunphy, having finished his meal, left the hut, and David followed him. The red-headed shepherd walked beside David, and gave him a few words of advice: "Ye'd betther go shtraight wid Jack Dunphy, me boy," he said in his husky brogue, "for 'tis himself 'ud put a bullet troo ye in a minnit, if he t'ought ye was crooked. D'ye see that?" - he pointed to his right car, more than half of which was missing - "he done that for me one day 'cause he t'ought I'd been talkin' about him to auld Montgomery's manager. Tuk his rifle, so he did, an' sint a half-ounce ball troo me ear. An' shure, if I had moved it wud have gone troo me hid. So be careful av Jack Dunphy, for he's aisy whin you're gain' his way, but he's the divil an' all whin he's crossed."

David Venn muttered an acknowledgment of the warning, and, taking the bridle of the brown horse, swung himself into the saddle.

Dunphy, who was already mounted, watched him with a critical eye. "Good job you can ride well," he said, approvingly. "It's nine o'clock now, and we've forty miles to go before morning - some of the roughest country in New South Wales, too."

But David Venn cared little for that. He had been reared in the Monaro country.

It was nine o'clock when Mitford and Mahoney took their lanterns and walked from the police camp to the bullock chain to call the roll, and remove the prisoners guilty of serious offences to their quarters for ... the night. The lanterns flashing on the chain showed that the two places at the end were empty. The birds had flown.

The troopers stared aghast and rubbed their eyes. None of the other prisoners could throw any light on the escape, although the university graduate grew quite voluble on the subject.

"By Gad, sir," he said excitedly to Mahoney, "the dashed-aw-fellah was vewy far fwom being so confoundedly-aw-souped up as he-aw-appeared to be. Upon my word of honah I heard him-aw-talking to that disreputable-aw-fellah that you-aw-anchored next to him on this-urn-confounded chain, and, by Gad, sir, I tell you he could-aw-talk as well as I can myself."

"Hould yer, gab,"said Trooper Mahoney menacingly; "shure I can't hear meself think. Wid yeo which way wud thim two blaggards be afther goin', Mitford?"

"Across the river, of course," said Mitford ruefully.

"This is a nice job I've got to report to the Commissioner. We'll have to be after them again at daylight."

The Commissioner spoke some choleric words when the crestfallen trooper told his story, but at once gave orders that no time was to be lost. The men must be recaptured at all costs. Already some very disagreeable remarks had been made in the metropolitan journals concerning the dastardly murder of a peaceable Italian subject on the Turon goldfields, and the Commissioner had been blamed for not affording sufficient police protection to persons engaged in their lawful avocations. Mr. Grey plainly foresaw that there would be a fresh outburst of hostile criticism when it became known that the suspected murderer had escaped from custody.

"Rouse up the black trackers at daylight," said the Commissioner with decision. "Take Mahoney with you, and don't come back here without the prisoners. I will send into Bathurst for extra police at once. 'Pon my soul, I don't know what things are coming to nowadays. That'll do, Mitford; you may go."

The trooper left the Commissioner's tent feeling decidedly

uncomfortable, but quite determined to follow Venn and Grogan to the ends of the earth if necessary. He knew that he could rely upon Jimmy and Jacky. They had traced David Venn all the way to Ponto's Island, and he was confident that they would be able to run their quarry down even more quickly on the second attempt. Besides how could Venn, when hampered with the companionship of that awful drunkard, maintain himself in those terrible ranges or win through to any place of refuge where he could get food and shelter? Escape under such circumstances was manifestly impossible.

Thus Bert Mitford argued with himself as he strode away from the Commissioner's tent, watching the lights of the camp-fires burning in the streets of the canvas city, and listening to snatches of song from singers gathered from lands afar. A few hours of troubled sleep, and he was awake again before the earliest of the eager gold-seekers who awoke with the first gleams of dawn.

Jimmy and Jacky grumbled considerably when aroused by the toe of Trooper Mitford's boot and made to understand that the white pfeller whom they had followed so long and so hard was away again, and that it was the order of the big boss that the pursuit should be taken up once more forthwith. But they had no toilette to make, and leaped from the bare earth on which they had been lying, ready at once for the business of hunting down any living creature upon whose trail they were set by an authority that they recognised.

Seeing the formidable nature of the country to be traversed-precipitous ranges for the most part, intersecting narrow gorges and valleys, in which flocks of scattered sheep found precarious pasture-Mitford decided that he and Mahoney would have to follow the black trackers on foot, until they ascertained the direction taken by the fugitives. Having located the line of flight, they could return for their horses as soon as practicable country was reached, and, by making a detour up the valley, avoid the precipitous ranges, and get on to the direct track when the country opened Gut again. Mitford reasoned that the runaways could not stay in the ranges, where nothing awaited them but starvation. They would have to make for some settlement in order to get food. He strongly suspected that David Venn would be inclined to make a break back to Bathurst, but what "that drunken fool of a Grogan" was likely to do puzzled him exceedingly.

Rousing Mahoney, the leader of the expedition made his simple preparations. He took blankets, a billy, and a gunny-bag full of rough tucker, dividing the light load between himself and his comrade, because the blacks, who were Queensland Myalls, only half tamed, were no good at all under burdens, and would have sulked for a certainty if compelled to carry them.

The song of the cradles, all along the banks of the Turon, was just beginning in the broadening dawn as the two white men and the two blacks waded through the shallow water in the same place where Dunphy and David had crossed not many hours before.

Jimmy and Jacky picked up the tracks easily in the soft ground, and, moving at a jog trot that made it hard work for Mahoney and Mitford to keep with them, they dashed into the light scrub that fringed the foothills of the ranges and breasted the ascent.

The sweat poured from the two white men as they toiled up the pathless track of the range in the wake of the blacks.

"Quite sure you're on the right track, .Iimmy?" said Mitford panting heavily, after half an hour of this strenuous climbing.

"My word," said Jimmy, with a grin that showed his glistening teeth. "Big white pfeller hold up lit pfeller here. Lit pfeller make plood, see." He pointed to a confused set of footprints on a patch of red clay, and to a darkened spot on a stone beside it.

"David Venn getting done," said Mitford to Mahoney, "an' I don't wonder at it. He must have been tired before he began. But this Grogan - if that is his real name - seems a pretty hefty kind of a chap. However, they can't be very far in front of us, and, as they took no tucker with them, we're bound to get them. I've never been up here before, but the country wouldn't keep a goat to the square mile by the look of it."

Mahoney saved his breath, and he wanted it, for he was a big man, and the climb was a severe strain. The two blacks plodded forward with every sign of assurance in their gait and gestures. Mitford realised that they were going over exactly the same ground as that taken by the fugitives.

"Why in t'under did them fellies come up this side av a house," grunted Mahoney, "instid of kapin' to the thraek, along the bank of the river?"

"That's just what has been puzzling me," said Mitford.

"We're out of the region of settlement altogether now - Hullo! Look out!" He dashed across to Mahoney and pushed him violently to the right as a huge boulder of granite, weighing something like a quarter of a ton, bounded down the side of the range, missing him by a few feet, and crashed down to the gorge below.

"By the hokey, that was a close call," said Mahoney, wiping his brow. "An' I hope there's' no more loose pebbles out of the same box, ayther,"

Mitford was frankly puzzled, and Jimmy and Jacky yabbered excitedly to each other for several minutes. They had hardly resumed their journey when another big boulder, leaping, bounding, dislodging clouds of dust, crashing through light scrub and ricochetting whenever it struck a solid rock, came heading straight for the climbers.

Mitford let out a warning yell and the four men jumped for their lives, but Jacky was a fraction of a section late. A scream rang out as the big boulder, like some maddened wild creature, charged down upon the luckless black tracker, and felled him to the ground. There was a sharp crack like a pistol shot as it passed, and poor Jacky lay on the earth, with his left leg broken below the knee.

8

The Red Cobber

"WELL, of all the cursed bad luck," said Mitford, savagely, as he bent down and satisfied himself that the leg was really broken, "this is the very worst. We can't leave Jacky here like this, and even if we could do so, I don't like the idea of going on without him. I'd better fix his leg up somehow, and then I suppose we'll have to carry him back to the camp."

The trooper hastily cut a small sapling and fashioned a rough splint, to which he bound the broken limb, while Jacky endured the agony of the jarring bone with stoical fortitude.

As Mitford was finishing this necessary job with Mahoney's assistance, a shout from the other blackfellow startled them, and looking up, they saw Jimmy gesticulating violently.

"Hi, boss," cried Jimmy, "big white pfeller sit down alonga rock, my word. Budgeree red cobber, boss."

"What's he meaning at all, at all ~" asked Mahoney.

"He says there's a big white man with a red head somewhere up in front of us," interrupted Mitford, "An' I suppose he's telling the truth. If he isn't I'll belt the life out of him in half a minute. Cobber means 'head' in the blacks' lingo."

He stood up, and, shading his eyes with the palm of his hand, directed his gaze up the side of the range that towered above him. Was it fancy or had he really caught a glimpse of a great shock of red hair disappearing behind a natural rampart of rock.

"I'll soon see who it is," exclaimed Mitford, drawing his revolver, and charging up the hill. "Come along, Mahoney."

The big Irishman kept close behind him, and together they

reached and climbed the rampart of rock. But there was no sign of the red-headed man.

The troopers found themselves looking down into a grassy hollow which nobody would have expected to find in such queer topographical surroundings. The hollow stretched away on the right, descending gradually into a narrow valley tufted with "I'm blessed if there isn't somebody here, too, Mahoney," said the leader, as he ran round to the little hut, revolver in hand, and pushed the door open.

There was nobody inside, but the sound of an axe, ringing upon timber, fell upon their ears, and together the two troopers rushed round to the side of the house and came face to face with Darby Kennedy, who was methodically splitting a log into handy lengths of firewood.

"Here, who the deuce are you 1 asked Mitford, displaying his horse pistol threateningly.

The huge red-headed man shook his head mournfully.

It appeared that he was either a semi-idiot or else that his hearing was defective.

"Ee the great cross of Croagh-Patrick. I'll make him hear me easy enough," said Mahoney, and, approaching the giant, he put his two hands together to make a speaking trumpet and shouted into the giant's ear, "What the blazes is yer name, an' what are ye doin' heer anyway?"

The big red head was slowly shaken from side to side with a gesture signifying hopeless non-comprehension.

"The deuce take the idiot. He's deaf and dumb," exclaimed Mitford angrily. "It's no good wasting any more time over him, Mahoney. We'll bring Jacky up here and leave him in charge of this fellow in the hut. I see that he has killed a sheep lately and has plenty of tucker. Then we'll push on with Jimmy, and when we have run down Grogan and Venn we can come back and carry Jacky down to the Turon, where he can get proper attention."

Just as Miftord had finished outlining his plan of campaign a cry from Jimmy put him on the "qui vive" again. He found Jimmy pointing excitedly to fresh hoof-prints in the turf.

The huge red-headed man appeared either a semi-idiot, or else his hearing was defective.

"One, two white pfeller sit down alonga here, bime by catchit horse, my word, ride helfaledder."

The trooper satisfied himself that the black tracker had unfolded the situation correctly. Climbing the rampart of rock behind the hut, he surveyed the lie of the country with a practised eye. Many hundred feet below him the Turon flowed in its narrow, winding gorge, but he could see where a horseman might strike out of the gorge, and, skirting the edge of the range, reach this long strip of tussocky grassland that bore away to the more open country in the north, That was the way the fugitives had gone, and that was the way that their pursuers must go too.

He explained the position to Mahoney in a few words, and then described what he proposed to do. Mahoney was to retrace his steps to the Turon, inform the Commissioner of the facts and get the horses. Riding his own and leading Mitford's and also a spare horse for Jimmy, he was to make his way without loss of time up the valley to a point which Mitford indicated. Then, striking westerly, he was to keep going until he reached the narrow grass strip that led to the more open country northwards. At that point Mitford, with Jimmy, would be waiting to meet him.

The red-headed man was standing within a few feet of Mitford while he was giving this explanation to Mahoney, and a glint of intelligence shot from the small muddy eyes. When Darby Kennedy looked up he saw Jimmy, the black tracker, regarding him with the keenest interest.

It was apparent that Jimmy, with his savage and primitive instinct, had discovered something that Mitford and Mahoney had missed. He disappeared into the hut, where Jacky, with his leg in the rude splints, lay on a bunk, and held a hurried guttural conversation with the invalid. Jacky intimated that he understood. He also reached one hand behind his back and slipped the sheath knife which was fastened to his belt round to the front.

"I'm going to leave Jacky here, with this red-headed dummy," said Mitford to Mahoney. "He won't take any harm for a couple of days, and I'll make that shepherd understand that he has to look after him, and give him tucker. And now, the sooner we're off the better."

So Mitford intimated by signs to Darby Kennedy - who had heard the whole conversation-that he was to look after the injured black tracker until the return of the police. Having done this, he set out on foot with Jimmy to follow the hoofmarks,. trying to account in his own mind for the presence of the horses at the hut. Mahoney started down the mountain with explicit instructions to meet his leader with the three horses atthe appointed rendezvous.

"I daresay the horses belonged to the run manager or the boundary rider," muttered Mitford to himself as he strode on behind Jimmy. "It's a pity the shepherd is a dummy. He could have explained the whole thing, and also how Ire came to let the two strangers ride away on the station horses. But once we get into the saddle with the tracks as fresh as this it won't be long before Jimmy runs them down."

Trooper and tracker travelled for a couple of miles along the gradually widening strip of tussocky country, with the ranges receding on their left and the strip of grassland running down towards the valley of the Turon. Late in the afternoon they saw a little cloud of dust approaching from the direction of the river. It was Mahoney, riding, and leading two spare horses.

The newcomer delivered a brief message from the Commissioner, directing Mitford to push on without delay.

"He's in a great rage intirely," said Mahoney, confidentially, "and when I told him about that red-headed dummy up in the ranges he shwore like a navvy, and said belike he was one of Jack Dunphy's spies. Did iver ye hear the like of that now! An' what wud Jack Dunphy be doin' up in them ranges anyhow, where there's nothing to shteal only gum trees?"

But Mitford grew thoughtful at once. Commissioner Grey was a very shrewd and experienced officer. Was it possible that the red-headed shepherd was not such a fool as he appeared to be? However, the best thing to do was to push on with all speed in the wake of the fugitives. When he had recaptured David Venn and Grogan there would be plenty of time to re-examine the shepherd and apply further tests in order to ascertain whether he was defective or merely a malingerer.

The horses were fresh and the two troopers and the black tracker went off at an easy canter, Jimmy" riding with only his big toe in the stirrup, after the fashion of the Queensland black police. He was a first-rate horseman, and the game of man-tracking was one that he thoroughly understood. For a couple of miles the hoofmarks of the two horses that had come from the hut were easily distinguishable, but then the country, though still open, became more stony, and Jimmy, who set the pace, had to slow up.

Before leaving the grassy strip of land he dismounted and made a careful examination of the hoofmarks that he had to follow, He pointed out the various peculiarities, a missing nail in one near fore shoe and a piece broken out of another, that rendered it possible for him to identify those particular set of marks among a thousand. A finger-print expert could not be more certain of his conclusions than Jimmy with those hoofmarks in front of him...

When he had finished drawing Mitford's attention to the hoofmarks, Jimmy volunteered an observation on another subject. "Red Cobber no dam good," he said, shaking his head.

"How's that, Jimmy?"

"T'row rock at Jacky," continued the tracker, with a gleam of savage anger in his chocolate-colored eyes.

"No, no; what the deuce makes you think that? No throw rock at Jacky. Rock fall by himself," Mitford took much trouble to assure Jimmy that his charges were unfounded, but the black obstinately maintained his opinion.

"Red Cobber gammon no can 'ear, no can yabber," continued Jimmy.

"You don't understand it, Jimmy," said Mitford. "Red Cobber is deaf and dumb, no can speak, no can hear, never no more."

"Red Cobber yabber all right," retorted Jimmy. "Only make gammon no can yabber."

"Don't you worry about that," said Mitford, with the easy confidence of a grown person directing a child. "Red Cobber look after Jacky till we come back."

"My word," said Jimmy, with his eyes flashing. "Mine bin tell Jacky. You look out for Red Cobber. Him t'row rock at Jacky. Him make gammon no can yabber! Jacky fix him no can yabber all ri'." He went on muttering to himself for a minute or two, and grinning horribly. Mitford began to have an uneasy feeling at the back of his mind. Was it possible that the red-headed shepherd had been shamming? He tried to dismiss the thought, but it hid pertinaciously in his brain and kept popping up most persistently all the afternoon.

After traversing about a mile of the stony ground the hoofmarks of the fugitives took a sharp, right-handed turn and swung into the open road leading to Jessie's corner. Jimmy could read the page of a dusty road as easily as the page of stony plain, and the pursuing party pressed on at a steady pace.

Meanwhile Dunphy and David Venn had made good use of their long start. Their horses were common bush-bred animals, but possessed of great powers of endurance. They kept up a loping canter that covered the ground at a very satisfactory speed, and the going had to be very rough indeed before the canter subsided into a walk.

As the two men travelled side by side along the open road to Jessie's Corner, David Venn was silent because he was preoccupied with thoughts of Esther, and Dunphy made no remarks because he was revolving in his mind the probability, amounting almost to a certainty, that they would be followed by police and black trackers. He knew the ability of the black trackers by bitter experience. rut he had baffled them before, and he hoped to baffle them again. Moreover, if Darby Kennedy got into the line of the pursuit the plans of the pursuers would surely be upset, and Darby Kennedy would find means to convey information to him by his elaborate system of "bush telegraphs," to the Honeymoon Inn at Jessie's Corner, whence it would be carried by a trusted hand to his refuge.

Jack Dunphy reckoned up the chances pro and con., but could not eliminate the probability that even at that moment they were being followed unerringly by the human sleuth hounds from Queensland and the troopers from Golden Point.

9

The Bishop's Adventure

IT was by this time nearly daybreak, and both horsemen were badly in need of a sleep. They had been travelling all night, and David was nearly worn out with fatigue even before he began the journey. Several times he nearly fell off his horse in sheer sleepiness. He mentioned the fact to Dunphy.

"We'll risk it," said Dunphy. "They can't track us by night, and I reckon we ought to be about ten hours ahead of them at least. Come along." He headed his horse off the road and into the bush, and David followed, ducking his head at the big branches, and fending off the light saplings with his hands.

When they had ridden nearly half a mile through the timber, Dunphy called a halt. The two men dismounted, tied their horses to two trees, curled themselves up on the bare ground, and in a minute or two were fast asleep. When they awoke, much refreshed by the sleep, the sun was shining brightly.

"We must push on," said Dunphy, looking anxiously at the sunlight filtering through the trees in their leafy retreat, "it must be eight o'clock at least."

So they mounted their horses again and emerged into the open road leading northwards.

"We've ten miles to go to Jessie's Corner," said Dunphy.

"I want to call there to see if there's any news from Darby Kennedy, and then we'll go right away to my den and lie low for a bit until they get tired of looking for us."

Dunphy spoke in tones of cheerful assurance, but in his inmost heart he kept revolving the conviction that the black trackers and police were after him. He looked up at the sky. It was blue and cloudless. No sign there of a friendly rainstorm to obliterate the tracks. He became silent and thoughtful. The two horses subsided into a very slow canter.

Then all at once, as they swung round a bend of the road, Jack Dunphy perceived two figures in front on horseback. They were two men and they rode one behind the other. A single glance told him they were not police. A second glance told him that the foremost of the two horsemen was a clergyman, and that the man who rode behind was probably his servant Both rode strong, upstanding, well-bred horses with manes and tails docked in the English fashion - evidently a pair of carriage horses, for they were both bright bay in color and perfectly matched.

A brilliant idea struck Jack Dunphy. "Our horses are pretty well used up," he said to Venn. "It's time we had a change of mounts. There they are in front of us. Keep up beside me till we draw level with his reverence there, and watch me give him the surprise of his life."

David Venn felt a sinking of the heart. So it had come at last. He was to take a share in an outrageous crime in the company of the notorious Dunphy. It was the first step of the career that he saw looming ever more distinctly before his eyes, a career into which he was driven not by any evil propensity of his own like the reckless dare-devil who rode by his side, but by that ironical fate which had decreed that the only way in which he could save the woman whom he loved from a shame that she in no way deserved was by associating himself with an outlaw and becoming a participator in that outlaw's crimes. David Venn had no wish to be a criminal. Strangely enough, he was forced into the position of taking part in a crime by the noblest emotion that can animate a man - the yearning to save a loved one from disgrace or even death.

His thoughts were roughly broken in upon by Jack Dunphy's voice crying, "You take the left side and I'll take the right. Come along, now."

David threw a startled glance at his companion and found that Dunphy had drawn a big horse pistol from the holster of his saddle, and was already quickening the pace of his horse with heel and voice. He urged his own horse forward and drew level with Dunphy. The clergyman and his servant were now no more than a hundred yards ahead and were travelling at a decorous walking pace.

After a keen survey of the strangers, David made a discovery, "The one in front is a bishop," he said, "a Protestant bishop. I've seen that queer looking kit before. Hullo, it's Bishop Troughton. He came up from Sydney .to preach at the Turon last Sunday. I saw a lot of the diggers going to the service, which was held in a big tent. And I saw the bishop afterwards in that very same rig-out - the gaiters, the hat, and all."

"Don't know much about bishops myself," grunted Dunphy, "but if he was the Archbishop of Canterbury I'd have that horse from him, quick and lively. A good cut of a horse he is, too, though a' lot too fat for my work. But I reckon I'll soon fine him down and make him forget his oarriage days. Now for it."

Dunphy hit his mount with his heel and the stones and dust flew up from the road as he and David Venn sailed along at a gallop and pulled their horses upon their haunches one on each side of the bishop.

"Hands up!" yelled Dunphy, and his appearance was so menacing that the good bishop immediately uplifted his two white and podgy little hands until he seemed to be in the act of bestowing a benediction upon his very surprising assailant. The groom who rode behind him turned a mottle greenish hue, and made no attempt to draw the ancient horse pistol which was stuck in his saddle.

"Man, I bid you reflect," began the bishop, who was not by any means without sturdy courage, "that this way of lawless violence can lead only to a shameful end in this world and to perdition in the next."

"Cut it," said Dunphy savagely, "and don't you play any game on me. Let's see what you've got in your fob!"

He plunged his left hand into the bishop's vest pocket while he held the pistol to his head with the right. The bishop, still holding his podgy hands on high, continued unavailingly to exhort the robber to turn from the paths of sin before it was too late.

Dunphy extracted a gold watch the size of a turnip from the bishop's fob and also a handful of silver, while his lordship vainly explained the terrors of eternal punishment, where the worm dieth not and the fire is not quenched, to the unconcerned sinner.

"Now then, I've no time to lose," said the robber brusquely "I and my mate are going to change horses with you and your servant." He pointed to a boulder at the side of the road. "You'll get off and stand on that rock, and you'll get on to my horse from it while I get on to yours. And your servant will change horses in the same way with my mate afterwards."

The good bishop protested with all the eloquence that had charmed large congregations down in Sydney. He recited the Sixth Commandment, a considerable portion of the Litany, and also the Collect for the day, but all without avail. Jack Dunphy was not a member of the Anglican Church, and ecclesiastical fulminations by any prelate of that church had no effect whatever upon him. "Get off!" he thundered, with a violent imprecation, and his lordship precipitately urged his horse towards the boulder and dismounted. With trembling fingers he essayed to unbuckle the girths.

"What are you doing that for 1" shouted Dunphy. "Surely you will allow me to take my own saddle," pleaded the bishop. "I have far to go and I cannot ride in a strange saddle by reason of the weakness of the flesh."

Dunphy cast a sharp glance at the bishop's saddle and saw that the saddlebags were bulging. "Just you leave that saddle where it is," he commanded, and his lordship stifled a sigh of disappointment.

A very brief examination showed that the bishop's saddlebags were stuffed with gold coin, small nuggets, and little chamois leather bags full of gold dust.

Dunphy's indignation knew no bounds. He held up a threatening forefinger at the bishop.

"Call yourself an honest man!" he shouted. "You wanted to rob me of that money by a mean, miserable trick. I've a good mind to put a hole through you." He held up his horse pistol threateningly, and his unfortunate victim made his pathetic explanation.

"That is not my money," he said. "It is the money of the Church, for whom I am but an unworthy steward. It represents the proceeds of the two collections taken last Sunday after morning and afternoon service in the big tent at the Turon."

"Well, it's mine now," said Dunphy with decision, as he

dismounted on the boulder beside the bishop. "Get up on my horse and give me yours."

The exchange was quickly effected, and David Venn having changed horses with the bishop's servant, his lordship was permitted to depart with his man - richer by a valuable experience of the wickedness of the ungodly, but poorer by the loss of many ounces of good Turon gold.

His lordship and his groom jogged along on their new mounts towards Jessie's Corner, where the bishop proposed to report his misadventure to the driver of the next mail coach, and insist upon the capture of the robbers and the recovery of the property of the Church. But Jack Dunphy and David Venn turned off the main road into a bush track, and the bishop's horse, feeling the grip of Dunphy's iron thighs and recognising the hands of a horseman on the bit, began his new experience. After the decorous solemnity of episcopal visitations, this bushranging was not without the charm of freedom. Dunphy's new mount kicked up his heels in exultation, and David Venn's big brown gave a couple of pig-roots in sympathy, without disturbing David in the least.

"Rattling fine pair of nags," said Dunphy, laughing.

"We'll strike out for the den now. Come on, I'll give you a go for it." The two horses broke into a gallop, and, with the wind singing in his ears, David Venn was carried along at furious speed into that new life with robbers and outlaws which he had not sought of his own choice, but which had been thrust upon him by his chivalrous act of self-sacrifice undertaken to save the honor and liberty of the woman he loved.

1 0

Jack Dunphy's Ruse

AS the two troopers and Jimmy the black-tracker trotted slowly along the open road in the wake of the fugitives, Mitford turned the events of the past few days over in his mind, and found them hard to fit together.

"David Venn was always a quite respectable young chap till he came to shoot that Dago, wasn't he, Mahoney?" inquired Mitford of his colleague, who was riding beside him.

"He was so," assented Mahoney. "I never see him do annything else only wurruk in his claim along o' that old Methody chap an' the boy."

"Oan't make out why he should have gone after Morosini with the gun an' shot him in the open in that cold-blooded way," grumbled Mitford. "No reason for it that I can see."

"Divil a bit of a reason at all, at all," assented Mahoney. "Then there's that drunken sweep, Grogan," continued Mitford. "He was so full of liquor that he couldn't speak when I saw him on the chain, yet when he escaped with David Venn he climbed that range all right, and even found a horse to ride away on. And Venn found another. I'd have bet my head I'd have had the pair of 'em within six hours, and now they're well mounted and a good bit ahead of us, and the Lord only knows when we'll get 'em."

"Shure 'tis the divil's own job intirely," agreed Mahoney, "an' me t'roat is as dry as a lime-burner's boot, so it is."

"Well, you won't get any beer this side of the Honeymoon Inn, at Jessie's Corner, if that's what you want," said Mitford, "so you had better keep your eye open for the nearest creek."

"I reckon I'm not that thirsty, anyhow," retorted Mahoney,

with dignity. "Shure I wondher now," he added, with cheerful irrelevance, "how poor Jacky is gettin' on wid that red-headed felly up at the hut - an' him wid the leg of him bruk, too, the poor hay then."

"Oh, Jacky will be all right," said Mitford confidently. "The shepherd will look after him, and when we get back there after landing our prisoners, we shall find Jacky perfectly well. It's wonderful how quickly blackfellows get over an injury that would almost settle a white man. A broken leg is nothing at all to them."

"I disremimber ever seein' that red-headed shepherd before," said Mahoney, lifting his cap in order to scratch his head. "I suppose, now, he wudn't be knowin' Grogan be anny chance!"

"Of course not," said Mitford impatiently. "How the deuce could he? The shepherd is deaf and dumb-and next door to idiotic as well, by the looks of him."

"Och, shure," said Mahoney, with a sudden gleam of intuition. "'Tis aisy enough to look idiotic. I do be misdoubtin' that red-headed mahn entirely."

Mitford was about to make a sharp reply to his obtuse comrade, when a cry from Jimmy arrested his attention. The black-tracker pointed out where the two fugitives had left the road, and turned into the bush to sleep. The troopers swung round, following Jimmy, and the three horses scrambled up the bank of earth at the side of the road and entered the light scrub of the bush. They followed the tracks for half a mile, and found where the runaways had camped.

"White pfeller sit down alonga here," announced Jimmy.

"Bimeby go sleep. Eimeby catchit horses an' go back dis way." He pointed to the hoofmarks in the soil, and showed Mitford the prints of the near fore shoe with the broken nail and of the off hind with the piece chipped off it.

"My word, Jimmy," said Mitford, encouragingly, "you budgeree tracker, no can make mistake, eh?"

"No fea'," said Jimmy proudly, as he led the party back to the road. Presently he pointed to another set of hoof-marks, that had cut into the road from a cross-track. These were the marks of the horses ridden by the bishop and his servant. Jimmy examined them carefully. "Him no hurry," he announced, "him plenty walk slow."

Next he discovered where Grogan and Venn had put their horses into a gallop to overtake the bishop. The two sets of tracks were confused near the boulder at the side of the road, but Jimmy patiently sorted them out. Unerringly he followed the tracks showing the broken nail in the near fore shoe of one horse and the piece chipped from the off hind shoe of the other.

"White pfeller goin' plenty slow now," he observed, noting that the horses had dropped to a walking pace. "Bimeby pretty soon catchit 'em."

He touched his own horse "rith his heel, and the animal shot forward, closely followed by Mitford and Mahoney.

Mile after mile went by in silence, and, at last, late in the afternoon, the troopers saw far off, at the side of the white road, the squat outline of the Honeymoon Inn, at Jessie's Corner. Four crossroads met at Jessie's Corner, and the Honeymoon Inn was a regular stopping place for the mail coach to and from Bathurst and the north.

Jimmy scanned the tracks intently. The hoofmarks that showed the broken nail in the near fore shoe of one horse and the piece chipped out of the hind of the other, indicated that the riders had put their mounts into a canter as soon as the Honeymoon Inn was in sight.

"Mine tinkit catchem all ri' bimeby soon," said Jimmy with a broad grin, pointing out the tracks in the soft going at the side of the road to Mitford.

Each trooper touched his horse with the spur, and approached the little roadside public house at a smart canter. The end of the chase was in sight at last, for there were the two horses that they had tracked all the way from the "Red Cobber's" hut on the mountains overlooking Golden Point. The animals were tied up to the fence alongside the Honeymoon Inn, and were standing there tired and dejected.

Jumping from their horses and drawing their pistols, Mitford and Mahoney dashed into the inn, and met old Joe Dunn, the proprietor, commonly known as "Ironbark Joe," in the passage.

"Hi, ye can't go in there!" yelled Ironbark Joe, as he saw the troopers making for the little private parlor opening off the passage on the opposite side to the bar.

"Come on; they're in here," said Mitford to Mahoney, elbowing

Joe Dunn aside most unceremoniously. The troopers, with their pistols cocked, burst into the little parlor - and found portly, Bishop Troughton eating a frugal meal of cold corned beef and potatoes, with his own man-servant standing behind his chair waiting upon him.

The bishop was so much astonished that he put down the glass that he was raising to his lips, untasted. It contained what Ironbark Joe called port wine.

"To what am I indebted -" he began with frigid politeness.

But Mitford, after one quick glance at the plethoric Churchman and his impassive man-servant, turned round to his comrade and remarked curtly, "Mahoney, we're sold."

The bishop's explanation, which was delivered with a great deal of rhetoric and many fulminations against the administration for the unsafe condition of the public roads, which enabled desperate and bloodthirsty villains to prey on travellers going about their lawful avocations, made clear to Mitford what had happened.

But still he could not understand how David Venn, the exemplary young miner, whose conduct was irreproachable up to the time of his quarrel with Morosini, could have become a bushranger. Still less could he understand how the wretched dipsomaniac who escaped along with Venn from the bullock chain could have either the inclination or the nerve to bail up a bishop and his servant on the high road in broad daylight, and take their horses from them as well as their money.

"Have you any idea, sir," said Trooper Mitford to the bishop, "who these men were who attacked you?"

"How can I know who they were?" said his lordship, testily. "All I can say is that I heard the younger man address the older and taller villain as 'Dunphy.'"

"Dunphy!" Trooper Mitford almost collapsed.

Mahoney's eyes goggled until they nearly came out on his cheeks. So the alleged dipsomaniac, whom Mahoney had put on the bullock chain, was the redoubtable Jack Dunphy, whose exploits were causing the Commissioner so much irritation.

Mitford sharply cross-examined the crest-fallen Mahoney about his captive, and quickly saw through Dunphy's ruse. Why, the villain must have descended from some den in the mountains for the express-purpose of robbing the Commissioner's tent, where the gold won by the miners was kept in large, iron-bound boxes, pending its despatch to Sydney under the care of the gold escort. Foiled in his purpose he had feigned drunkenness, and would have been released from the chain and sent about his business, even if he had not escaped with David Venn.

"What'll the Commissioner say when he hears that we had Jack Dunphy on the chain, an' let him get away?" asked Mahoney, dolefully. But his question remained unanswered.

Trooper Mitford questioned the bishop closely about the two men who had attacked him, and the choleric ecclesiastic gave a moderately clear account of his misfortunes. The villains had got away with his two best carriage horses, valuable animals, that were as good in saddle as in harness. They were a well-bred pair, with plenty of bone and substance, and they could not be replaced for less than a hundred guineas. The scoundrels had also taken his gold watch and chain, and rough gold and coin to the value of about £200, the proceeds of two collections taken during morning and afternoon service at the Turon. That amount, he explained, was the property, not of himself, but of the Church, and he should instruct the Colonial Secretary, on his return to Sydney, that the men who carried it off were guilty of the crime of sacrilege, as well as robbery - a fact which would, he hoped, be remembered by the judge who would have to sentence them eventually.

Mitford groaned audibly at the close of his harangue.

He foresaw that it might be some time before Jack Dunphy and David Venn were caught. They had acquired two first-rate horses and a sum in gold which would enable them to buy assistance and shelter from many of the shadier class of small settlers in the remote bush.

But it was Dunphy's master stroke of audacious cunning that annoyed Mitford the most. The bushranger's idea of changing horses with the bishop, and of so managing it that no tell-tale human footmarks should appear in the road for the black tracker to decipher, had completely fooled both the infallible black-tracker and the two troopers who were guided by him. Jimmy, the tracker, had performed his task with unwearying pertinacity. He had followed the broken horseshoe and the shoe with the missing nail, from the Red Cobber's hut overlooking the gorge of the Turon, to the Honeymoon Inn, at Jessie's Corner, a distance of close upon fifty miles. But the pursuit had been baffled by Dunphy's ingenuity in making his lordship the bishop unwittingly the means of leading the police astray and enabling the daring robber and his companion to make good their escape. The troopers had followed the right horses, but they had got the wrong men!

"No good," said Mitford, stamping his foot with ill-suppressed disappointment. "But I'm not beaten yet. We'll ride back to the point where the other two horses left the road and entered the bush. Jimmy can follow their tracks as easily as he can follow these. I'll run them down if I have to follow them for a week."

But a short halt for rest and refreshment was absolutely necessary. The horses also had to be fed. Mitford summoned Ironbark Joe, and ordered him to take the horses round to the yard and give them a feed of corn. The innkeeper went away, with a sinister gleam in his horribly squinting eyes, to carry out his instructions, and Mitford and Mahoney left the bishop to finish his meal, with no solace other than his own bitter reflections, while they repaired to the fly-infested dining-room of the Honeymoon Inn for a hasty dinner. As for Jimmy, the black-tracker, he was provided with a meat bone and a hunk of bread, which he ate, sitting on his heels on the verandah.

When the situation was explained to Jimmy, he grinned cheerfully. "Mine tinkit track no good bimeby Boon," he observed oracularly, pointing at the same time to the sky. The sky was blue and almost cloudless, but Jimmy's black forefinger indicated a 'small "mackerel" patch far away to the south.

"The lazy black divil do be wantin' anny old excuse to lave off wurruk," remarked Mahoney, mopping his brow with a big blue handkerchief. "Shure, 'tis as hot as the hobs of hell this minit, an' why wudn't he find the tracks as aisy as he did this mornin'?"

Mitford shot a questioning glance at Jimmy. He was aware that these Queensland aboriginals required to be handled carefully, and that though wonderfully clever in the bush, they lacked patience and perseverance in following up a long task. But Jimmy seemed perfectly good-tempered, and ready to go on. He pulled away at his black clay pipe, and scrutinised the sky carefully, looking all round the horizon.

"Mine tinkit rain coming bimeby," he remarked briefly.

"How soon bimeby?" queried Mitford.

The aboriginal grinned, and touched his pipe with his forefinger. Then he held up all the fingers of one hand first, and next all the fingers of the other.

"He says one would have time to smoke ten pipes of bacca before the rain comes," interpreted Mitford, "that is to say, three or four hours, at any rate,"

Jimmy grunted, and nodded his head vigorously. "T'ree foh hours all ri'," he muttered corroboratively.

"So I reckon we'd best make a start," said Mitford. "It's four o'clock now. We ought to be able to see which way they've gone, at any rate, before the rain comes."

As he went round to the yard at the back, where the horses were feeding, old Ironbark Joe, of the squinting eyes, hastily retired into the house. He emerged in answer to Mitford's "Hullo," and the trooper paid him for the meals and horsefeed. Ironbark Joe went away, chuckling horribly to himself, as the troopers and the black-tracker mounted and rode back along the road that they had already travelled,

"My horse is a bit sore in front," remarked Mitford, after he had ridden a few hundred yards. "Stiff, I expect, after his journey this morning. But it will wear off when he gets warm."

"Begad, my baste is tindher, too," said Mahoney anxiously. "I can feel him give undher me ivery time he puts his fut down."

"Shake him up into a canter," said Mitford, touching his own horse with the spur.

But the lameness of both was even more pronounced when cantering than when trotting, and instead of getting better, and throwing off the lameness, they got rapidly worse. Jimmy's mount was going splendidly, in marked contrast with the horses ridden by the troopers. The black, who was still sucking at his short clay pipe, looked 'round inquiringly at Mitford, and pointed to the sky.

"It's no good, Jimmy," said Mitford, thoroughly vexed and worried. "My horse is dead lame."

"An' shure, so is mine," added Mahoney, whose mount was limping painfully.

They were only three miles from the Honeymoon Inn, and Mitford decided, much against his will, that. the only thing to do was to return there and endeavour to get fresh horses.

Slowly and painfully the lame horses limped back, while the troopers walked beside them. " Mitford lifted up the lame fore foot of his own horse and examined it closely, but could detect nothing amiss. Nor could he find the cause of the trouble in Mahoney's horse.

They just reached the inn at Jessie's Corner as the storm broke, the wind swinging round to the south, and the rain falling in a drenching, driving downpour.

Jimmy put his clay pipe in his pocket, regretfully.

"No can track bimeby," he remarked. "No can catchit white pfeller. Budgeree rain, my word, make no can see tracks."

And Mitford felt in his inmost heart that the black told the truth. The rain and the horses' lameness together had made further pursuit hopeless. He would have to make many wide casts now before picking up the scent again.

Late that night, when the troopers were asleep in the inn, and Jimmy was safely curled up in the straw in the cowshed, Ironbark Joe passed like a shadow to the open stalls, where the two lame horses stood side by side, each resting the injured fore foot. He carried a pair of carpenter's pincers in his hand. He went first to Mitford's horse, a fine, upstanding black, and, lifting up the lame foot, dug out a small piece of clay from the centre of the frog of the hoof. Underneath the piece of clay was the head of a large nail. Ironbark Joe clamped his pincers to the nail and pulled it out. It was fully three inches long. He stuck the bit of clay over the hole, and put down the foot again. He repeated the operation in every detail with Mahoney's horse. Then, like, a shadow, he flitted back to the house.

At daybreak Mitford got up and went to look at the horses. They were standing fair and square, distributing their weight equally on each leg. He took them both out of the stalls. They walked with scarcely a trace of lameness.

"Just as I thought," said Mitford to Mahoney. "The journey yesterday was a bit too much for them. The rest has put them all right, and we'll be able to ride back to the Turon. I don't like facing the

Commissioner without taking Venn and Dunphy back with me, but there's nothing else to be done. If the horses hadn't gone lame we'd have picked up the tracks before the rain came. We've done our befit, but the luck is against us."

"Shure, it is, indade," echoed Mahoney, ruefully, "an' 'tis my belafe there's more throuble comin' shtill out av this day's wurruk be rason av his riverince in the house beyant. He's so mad wid bein' robbed, that I misdoubt if he won't raise the Guv'ment on us. Annyway, be the bleasin' av hivin, shure it might 'ave been worse."

"How's that?" asked Mitford, considerably mystified. "Shure, 'tis only a Prodestan' bishop he is afther all." said Mahoney.

11

The House in the Tunnel

ANYONE who has travelled north of Bathurst, where the rivers and creeks have been scored and pitted for mile after mile by the diggers, and where the heaps of brown and yellow clay still remain to testify to the feverish activity generated in humanity by that "*auri sacra fames*," that "accursed hunger for gold," which was not less keen in the fifties in Australia than in Europe in classical times, knows -how precipitous, how tumbled, and how grotesquely irregular are the mountains in that region.

Piled high by some outburst of volcanic force, sliced and intersected by the action of the water, flattened into gaunt plateaux by the force of denudation, which have lopped off the peaks and rounded off the shoulders, these ranges contain every imaginable variety of fantastic outline. Steep precipices overhanging dark and inaccessible gullies abound. In some cases the opposite sides of the gully are far apart and the thickly timbered gully resembles a valley which might conceivably be cleared and even tilled. In other cases the opposing precipices are so close together that the gully, seen from above, becomes a mere slit in the primeval rock - a slit, moreover, that is invisible at a distance of a hundred yards.

In the huge towering mass of rock which was known locally as Mount Elephant there was such a slit as this. five hundred feet in height from the entrance at its base, this narrow rocky slit roofed with a living thatch - a thatch of sassafras and acacia, peppermint and grass-trees, and a score of other growths that had rooted themselves into the shallow soil, and grown bending forward on either side and interweaving their branches and foliage until they made an impenetrable covering that shut out sun and wind and rain, and made the narrow gorge a covered tunnel between the valleys on either side of the range of which Mount Elephant formed part.

This tunnel hewn out of the rock by Nature herself and roofed by her hand with a tangled plant-growth, knitted so closely as to be impervious to all weather influences, was about a quarter of a mile in - length. Neither of the entrances was more than a yard in width, though the tunnel became wider inside, and loose brushwood, easily detached by those who knew the secret, closed them both. Once inside this covered gorge the curious investigator might observe a whole series of immense concavities in the living rock on either side-concavities fashioned uncounted ages ago by the action of water. These concavities were arranged irregularly on either side of the gorge.

About eighty yards by actual measurement from the eastern end of the gorge or covered tunnel it happened that a concavity in the northern wall was situated exactly opposite a similar concavity in the southern wall. The result of this fortuitous disposition by Nature was that a person walking through the gorge entered a high vaulted chamber having an exit at either end into the tunnel - an exit no more than three feet in width. By blocking up these exits with a strip of canvas a place of abode, which was cool in the hottest summer and which could be warmed by a fire in winter, was quite simply provided. No architect or contractor had a hand in constructing this unique dwelling.

Jack Dunphy was the occupier of the house in the tunnel, and he held it rent free.

On a certain night of August, 1851, five men were assembled in Jack Dunphy's den. The party consisted first of Jack Dunphy himself; secondly, of his first lieutenant, Tom Warburton, who had made his way back to the den by means known only to himself after the escape of his chief from the bullock-chain at Golden Point; thirdly, of Bill Rogers, a truculent, black-brewed individual of great activity but limited intelligence; fourthly, of Charles Russell Fitzroy Stanhope, a tall slight man with a long, fair moustache, and a pronounced English accent; and fifthly, of David Venn, a duly accredited member of the association, who had been personally introduced by the president.

Stanhope was smoking a good cigar and reading a copy of a Sydney weekly newspaper a month old. Rogers was smoking a short, black pipe and staring gloomily into the big log fire set at the open entrance of the cave on the leeward side. The other three were sitting on the ground playing cut-throat euchre. It was nine o'clock at night, and the dark mound outside was as silent as a sepulchre.

In the act of dealing a grimy pack of cards Dunphy paused and listened intently. The sound of footsteps groping along the tunnel at the eastern end was faintly heard by all the men. Instantly they sprang to their feet.

Dunphy seized a double-barrelled shot gun that stood in the corner beside his own rude bunk of dried leaves covered with a kangaroo-skin rug. "Who's there?" he yelled. "Answer or I'll blow you to pieces."

An awful sound like the moan of a wild beast in pain came from the dark depths of the tunnel beyond the range of the glow from burning logs.

A panic of superstitious terror fell upon the men in the den. Yet Dunphy stood firm, holding his gun to his shoulder. He feared the unknown visitant who had come to his secret stronghold out of the immense solitudes of the untraversed mountains and valleys. He feared - but he held his ground. Whether the stranger was a man or devil he knew not, but he stood ready to fire as soon as the disturber came into the radius of the log-fire's light.

Moments passed. The unearthly moaning was repeated with a tone of agonised beseeching in it. The four other men stood behind Dunphy grasping their pistols. If the intruder was mortal, and hostile, he had small chance of leaving the tunnel alive. That at least was plain.

The light from the fire flickered and glowed, illuminating the stark rock face at either side of the tunnel with fitful gleam. And suddenly, out of the black darkness into the red circle of the light, there scrambled, with hesitating steps, the figure of a man - but a man of such terrifying aspect that the spectators were appalled. His coarse matted shock of long red hair fell around his face, and his eyes looked out from the hair with a glare of insanity. His huge cavernous mouth was wide open, and from it came a sound which was like nothing that those men had ever heard before. He pointed to his mouth with the forefinger of a hand that was like a great hairy paw.

It was the Red Cobber.

"By the Lord it's Darby Kennedy!" exclaimed Dunphy, and dropped his gun. "What's the matter with you," he almost screamed in the over-powering nervous tension that affected the horror-stricken assemblage.

But Darby Kennedy only groaned again, and pointed to his mouth.

"By all the saints in Heaven," cried Dunphy, "there is no tongue in the man's mouth. It has been cut out at the root."

The Red Cobber nodded his great head despairingly.

He staggered into the den and fell down on the dry leaves that made a carpet on the bare rocky floor.

Jack Dunphy poured some rum from a bottle into a pannikin and filled it up with water. He held it to the lips of the maimed wretch, and Kennedy swallowed it greedily. The men who clustered round saw that the shepherd's red hair was stained a deeper red on the top. There was a terrible smashing wound on the apex of the skull, but the skull was thick. It had evidently resisted a blow that would have crushed an ordinary skull like an eggshell.

To every question the shepherd's only answer was the same eerie, blood-freezing moan that the men had first heard out of the darkness.

Darby Kennedy could not write for he had never learned how to do so. He could not speak because his tongue was gone. Therefore, he had no means of communicating with the awed and horror-stricken men except by gestures. He set himself to act the tragedy of which he had been made the victim.

First he lay down on Dunphy's pile of rugs, closed his eyes and simulated sleep.

"He was asleep when it happened," said Stanhope, who had the quickest brain of the gang, and at once assumed the office of interpreter.

Darby Kennedy nodded his great wounded head in token that the interpretation was correct. Then he picked up a heavy billet of wood that stood near the fire, part of the fuel that had been made ready for burning. With the billet of wood he aimed a heavy blow at the pile of rugs on which he had been lying.

"Somebody hit him on the head with a club while he was asleep," translated Stanhope, and again the red head nodded slowly.

Darby Kennedy drew a sheath knife from his belt, bent over the pile of rugs, pointed to his mouth, and slashed at the air with his keen blade.

"He means to say," said Stanhope, "that after he had been stunned by a blow, the assailant cut out his tongue with a sheath knife."

Again the Red Cobber nodded his head despairingly. "But who was the man who did it?" asked Dunphy. The Red Cobber evidently knew, but the Red Cobber could not communicate his knowledge, for every avenue of communication was closed to him seeing that he could neither speak nor write.

The log fire lit up the concave walls of the house in the tunnel, and threw into bold relief the faces of the men who stood around this living but mutilated enigma.

Stanhope was the first to speak. "Judging by the nature of the attack," he said, "I imagine it was not made by a white man. It must have been made by a savage, presumably a blackfellow. It's a kind of thing a blackfellow might do in a frenzy of revenge."

Darby Kennedy nodded again. The tall man with the golden moustache had guessed right.

"I never heard of any blackfellow being in these mountains," said Dunphy. "They disappeared long ago."

Darby Kennedy listened intently. Then he moved rapidly round the den, bending forward and peering on the ground.

"It was a black-tracker who attacked him," interpreted the quick-witted man with the golden moustache. Now we can reconstruct the whole affair. Kennedy was asleep, no doubt in his own hut on the mountains overlooking Golden Point, forty miles away from here, when a black-tracker hit him on the head with a club and then, while Kennedy was still stunned, cut out his tongue.

The shepherd went down on his hands and knees on the ground and crawled slowly round the den dragging his left foot after him.

"The black-tracker had his left leg broken," added the interpreter.

Gradually Jack Dunphy and David Venn also began to under-

understand what had taken place. One of the two black-trackers who had traced Venn to Ponto Island had evidently followed him again when he escaped for the second time. The black, who was, no doubt, accompanied by his mate, for they always worked in pairs, and who was also closely followed by troopers, came to Darby Kennedy's hut. His leg had been broken, possibly in an encounter with the shepherd, and the black in revenge had stunned Kennedy with a waddy and then, for some incomprehensible reason, had mutilated him by hacking out his tongue-perhaps to prevent him from informing against his barbarous assailant.

"There were two trackers and two troopers at the police camp," said David Venn. "The black who did this must have done it unknown to the troopers. Therefore, they must have gone away before it happened. The question is, where are they now - the second black and the two troopers."

"They're after us, I expect," said Dunphy grimly, and again the shepherd nodded his great wounded head.

So they had the whole story at last, or, at any rate, as much of it as they were likely to be able to extract from Darby Kennedy.

"Anyhow we are safe for the present," remarked Stanhope. "The rainstorm last night must have completely blotted out the tracks. There isn't a black in Australia who could follow a horse's hoof-marks after a storm like that."

Dunphy was rather inclined to take the same view, although he could not help feeling a trifle anxious when he realised that a human bloodhound - the mate of the savage who had dealt so terribly with Darby Kennedy - was on his trail, with a couple of troopers as well armed and as courageous as any outlaw of the bush in support.

A rapid calculation of times and distances showed him that when the black with the broken leg had managed to escape after mutilating Darby Kennedy so frightfully the shepherd must have travelled the intervening forty miles that lay between his hut and the den with which he was well acquainted. He must have performed that journey across the mountains on foot, an extraordinary achievement for a man suffering from such ghastly injuries.

Meanwhile the Red Cobber was looking round the den with ravenous eyes. He saw a big case of hard biscuits in one corner, and seizing one of the biscuits he broke it in pieces and soaked it in the remainder of the rum and water which was in the pannikin. He devoured the biscuit, thus softened, with manifest haste.

"The poor devil won't be able to eat meat or any hard tack for days," said Stanhope. "The wound at the root of his tongue is still raw."

The gang watched Darby Kennedy with fascinated interest and talked over the dreadful episode in low whispers. But Dunphy spoke up at last.

"Well boys," he said, "Darby Kennedy was a good friend to us when he was outside, and I reckon it won't do us any harm to have him with us now."

"What do you mean, exactly?" asked the tall man, as he stroked his golden moustache and surveyed the mutilated giant reflectively.

"I propose," said Dunphy, "to make him one of the gang."

There was a low hum of assent, and David Venn realised, with a feeling that was more than half abhorrence, that he had gained one more associate in the person of the red-headed giant who would certainly stop at nothing in order to wreak his revenge upon the police as well as upon their black satellite, who had maimed him so fiend¬ishly and so irretrievably.

Thus David came to understand that self-sacrifice as well as adversity may make one acquainted with strange bedfellows.

1 2

The "Waddy Mudoia"

ESTHER PENNYCUICK went about her work at the claim like a girl in a dream for a couple of days after the disappearence of David Venn.

Old Malachi, in order to retain possession of the claim, was obliged to work it with four persons on account of the measurement. So he took in a partner to replace Venn. The new partner was Malcolm M'Lachlan - the same young Scotsman who had sung "Annie Laurie" so sweetly on that evening which seemed to Esther to be a hundred years in the past - so many terrible things had happened since then. M'Lachlan took up Venn's job of feeding the hopper of the cradle with the washdirt. Esther kept the machine in constant motion. She scarcely spoke a word from morning to night.

"Nice looking lad, but sulky," said M'Lachlan to himself, and devoted himself to his pipe. He began to regret having joined the Cornishman's party. If the lad was sulky, the old man was moody and morose, with long silences, broken by violent explosions of rage during which texts from the Hebrew prophets were hurled red-hot at anyone who dared to interrupt. It seemed that the sulky boy was the only person who had any influence over Malachi at these times. M'Lachlan retired to his own tent at night, feeling irritated by a tension and a sense of mystery about the demeanour of the sulky lad and the morose old man. It seemed to the newcomer that the sullen behaviour of his two mates was not sufficiently explained even by the fact that his predecessor had shot a prowling Dago, doubtless for very good reasons.

It was small wonder that Esther Pennycuick was very silent in those bitter days. With the object of saving her from degradation, humiliation, imprisonment, and perhaps worse things, her lover had taken the guilt of shooting Morosini upon his own shoulders. And she had let him take it. Moreover, he had escaped from custody, not for his own sake, but for hers, in order that the deception might not be discovered by the officers of the law, and in order that an obstacle might be placed in the way of that full investigation at a trial which would inevitably result in the disclosure, at any rate, that she, a woman, was living among men and masquerading as a man.

Esther Pennycuick yearned passionately for David Venn, and hated herself not less passionately for having let him go. Her conscience was sorely troubled. But what was done could not be undone. Once the thread of the event had. been woven by Time into his fabric, it could never be released. It had become part of the very stuff and substance of Destiny. She turned to old Malachi in order to distract her mind from the subject of David Venn-in order to drown the thoughts that were maddening her.

"Father," she said to the old man on the evening of the first day after David's departure, "are you feeling better now."

"Ay," mumbled the old man. "God is my strength and power. I have pursued mine enemies and destroyed them, and turned not again until I had consumed them. And I have consumed them and wounded them that they could not arise. Yea, they are fallen under my feet."

Esther groaned in despair. Was it always to be like that? She looked for sympathy and support, and she got nothing but the ravings of incipient religious mania.

Next morning she got up at dawn, put on her blue shirt and moleskin pants and heavy boots, and walked down to the river. The water had fallen, and at the ford she hardly wetted her feet as she crossed. That was the way that David had taken. She felt that she must get away by herself and think things out. She would climb the range by the track that David had used. And, perhaps, if she could analyse the whole maddening puzzle by herself on the mountainside, she might be able to find a solution of the problem that beset her-the problem of her duty, which was so frightfulfrightfully complicated by her love, not only as a woman, but as a daughter. She took a bottle of milk and some bread and meat with her.

As she climbed the side of the range just after daybreak, trying to smooth out the tangled skein of circumstance, and to solve the doubts that assailed her heart and conscience, she became dimly aware of some wild creature moving through the scrub beside her. Probably a kangaroo or wallaby, she reflected, with momentarily arrested attention. And yet the creature, whatever it was, seemed to move too slowly for one of the big marsurpials. She paused in her climb and fixed her eyes on the low, bushy scrub which undulated perceptibly as the animal crawled through it.

Ha! The creature was coming straight towards her.

Esther Pennycuick began to get really frightened. Suppose it was an enormous snake. She had not been long in Australia. She knew very little about the animals of the bush, and, for she was aware of to the contrary, there might be creatures in these solitudes which were both powerful and dangerous.

All at once the scrub parted, and a dark form wriggled slowly and painfully out of it, and stopped almost at her feet. Esther sprang back in dismay.

Certainly Jacky the black-tracker was not a reassuring sight. His shirt and pants were in rags. He was hauling himself painfully along the rough ground by slow stages. And his broken left leg dragged uselessly behind him. It was still lashed to the stout sapling that Trooper Mitford had converted into a splint, but the jarring of the ends of the bone must have given the aboriginal the most acute agony. He bore it stoically. Jacky was consumed by a raging thirst. He had not touched food or drink for rwenty-four hours - in fact, not since he had wreaked his savage vengeance on the Red Cobber, and, leaving his victim lying insensible in the hut, had crawled away with the intention of getting back to the police camp at the Turon, where, at least he was sure of his rations.

When the black-tracker saw Esther Pennycuick, his eyes met hers with a dumb appeal.

"Gib Jacky water," he said in a husky whisper. Esther had no water to give him, and there was none nearer than the river. But she had her bottle of milk and, going down on her knees beside the black, she placed the neck of the bottle in his mouth and tilted it up. Jacky swallowed the milk in long gulps, and his voice returned to him.

"Gotten damper!" he inquired anxiously.

Esther had no damper, but she had bread and meat, and she gave the food to Jacky, who devoured it with quick snaps, like a dingo. He looked at her gratefully.

"Now tell me where you came from, and how you got your leg broken, and who bound it up for you like that?"

So Jacky told her as well as he was able, and she learnt that he was one of the black-trackers who were taken out by Trooper Mitford to hunt David Venn. She recoiled from the black with horror. She had given him food and drink, although he had been doing his best to run down her lover, till some accident occurred by which his leg had been broken, and he had been compelled to desist.

But Esther Pennycuick's womanly compassion reasserted itself. The black was not really her enemy. He had only been doing what he was told to do by those who gave him food and expected him to give them service in return for it.

The aboriginal was enduring terrible sufferings, and she had helped him already. She could not leave him there. In spite of his vigorous savage nature, it was more than likely that he would never reach Golden Point alive if she did.

"Can you crawl along now if I stay with you?" asked Esther.

"Mine tinkit," said the black eagerly, and he began his painful journey once more, moving like a wounded snake.

But the exertion and the pain were too much for him, and he came to a stop after going a few yards.

"Waddy mundoia no good," muttered Jacky, looking at Esther with pathetic eyes, and tapping the sapling to which the broken leg was firmly lashed.

Esther dimly comprehended that "Waddy mundoia" meant woooden leg in Jacky's native language. Alas! the black-tracker's "Waddy mundoia" could not be removed without the worst results, but Esther thought she saw a way out of the difficulty. She helped Jacky up on to his sound leg, and she supported him with her arm while he made his way, one-legged, down the side of the range. It was difficult and dangerous work. There were moments when Esther thought that both of them would be pitched headlong to the bottom of the mountain. But she stuck to her task, and she crossed the shallow river at last with her charge, encouraging him with cheering words as they went along and thus helping him to endure the agony caused by the jarring of the two ends of the broken bone.

When she reached the police camp Esther was nearly worn out herself, but she helped Jacky to his gunyah. which he shared with Jimmy, who was still absent on the hunt, and Jacky subsided upon his straw with a guttural grunt of relief while Esther made ready to notify the police camp of the return of the lost auxiliary. But she received the surprise of her life before she left the black-tracker's gunyah.

"Mine tinkit," said Jacky, looking at her with a twinkle in his eye, "you make budgeree big gammon. You not boy. You white Mary."

Yes, Jacky had read her secret. She was, indeed, a "white Mary"- the aboriginal expression for any and every white woman. In a panic she besought Jacky not to reveal her secret.

"All ri', White Mary," said Jacky, submissively, and looking at her with dog-like fidelity. "Jacky no yabber White Mary make gammon." And she knew that he would keep his word. But Jacky, overcome by such kindness as he had never experienced in his life, then and there became Esther Pennycuick's devoted and most faithful adherent, and resolved, in his savage soul, to serve her and her only, to the end.

Next day Mitford and Mahoney with Jimmy the tracker returned to the Turon disappointed and discomfited. Mitford's interview with the Commissioner was a trying one, for Commissioner ·Grey did not select his words so as to spare his listener's feelings when he felt that he had just cause for indignation.

"You had this man Dunphy - a fellow who has committed every crime in the calendar - actually in custody," he stormed, "and you allowed him to escape along with this dangerous murderer, Venn, and bail up his lordship, the bishop, who lunched with me here only last Sunday and complimented me upon the orderliness of the encampment and the admirable security of the district. Moreover you allowed yourself to be tricked by a pair of stupid louts like Dunphy and Venn so that they

Jacky then and there became Esther Pennycuik's devoted and most
faithful adherent.

got away into the mountains, leaving no trace of their whereabouts. And finally my best black-tracker has come back with a broken leg that will render him useless to me for weeks, and with a confused story that he received the injury at the hands of some unknown scoundrel whom he calls the Red Cobber, and in whose care you appear to have left him. It seems to me, Mitford, that you have made a dreadful mess of the whole business."

The trooper took his gruel without flinching. "I'm afraid I've made mistakes, sir," he admitted, "but the luck went dead against us. But I'll get Dunphy and Venn yet, if it costs me my life."

"Tut-tut, man, don't talk rot about it costing you your life," said the Commissioner. "When once you come up with these vulgar scoundrels you'll find that they'll surrender fast enough. And now, I want you to come with me to the black-trackers' camp. I should like to question Jacky myself about that shepherd in the hut. It seems to me more than likely that he was a friend and ally of Dunphy's, and that he rolled those rocks on top of you on purpose, with the object of wiping out Dunphy's pursuers *en bloc*."

"Very good, sir," said the crestfallen trooper, and, as he walked beside the Commissioner to the black. trackers' camp, he had to admit to himself that he had been far too confiding in accepting the drunken Grogan and the imbecile dummy of the shepherd's hut at their respective face values.

Dr. Curtis, a young medical student, who had deserted a good practice in Older to go to the diggings, had fixed up Jacky's broken leg very effectively, and Jacky was lying on a heap of straw in his gunyah when the Commissioner called.

Jacky had no objection to relate some of his experiences.

He answered the Commissioner's questions glibly enough, and mentioned that Jimmy had actually seen the Red Cobber rolling the rocks down on top of them as they climbed. Jacky went on to declare that he had suffered. much pain from his "waddy mundoia," and consequently, when the Red Cobber was asleep, he escaped from the hut. He had a bad night on the mountains, but in the early morning he met "Jacka Penkik," who had helped him baek to the camp.

The story was fluent enough, but there were gaps in it and it was unconvincing. Moreover, Jacky showed a marked disinclination to discuss the subject of the Red Cobber, and always shied off when the Commissioner tried to exact some definite information about the shepherd. Commissioner Grey was vaguely dissatisfied with the result of the interview, and strongly suspected Jacky of concealing the truth.

Just as he was about to leave the gunyah the Commissioner noticed round Jack's neck a string of bark fibre from which depended some object that was hidden under Jacky's shirt. The Commissioner became inquisitive. He inquired as to the nature of the object which Jacky guarded with such care. Jacky temporised, but finally admitted under pressure that it was a very potent charm given to him by an elder of his tribe in Queensland with strict instructions that it was never to be shown to a white man or evil would befall the' wearer.

But the Commissioner was unsympathetic. He demanded to see the object. Very reluctantly Jacky produced it - a small bag, very neatly made of plaited grass.

The Commissioner lifted the string off Jacky's neck and held the small bag of plaited grass in his hand. There was something in it. He turned the bag upside down on the bottom of an upturned candle-box which formed the 'sole article of furniture in Jacky's abode. Out dropped a dirty brown object of unpleasant appearance.

"Why the devil is he carrying this thing round his neck?" exclaimed the mystified Commissioner.

"Dat bery good magic," said Jacky sullenly. "Dat belonga Red Cobber. Red Cobber made big gammon no can yabber. Jacky fix 'im no can yabber all ri'."

The Commissioner and the trooper stared with horror at their aboriginal auxiliary but their was no doubt any longer that Jacky was telling the truth.

"I feel certain that this Red Cobber as Jacky calls him is an accomplice of Dunphy's," said the Commissioner as soon as he had escaped from the dreadful gunyah and Trooper Mitford had to admit that the indications were in favour of the supposition.

"In which case;" said the Commissioner briefly, "we may expect bitter reprisals."

By direction of the Commissioner Trooper Mitford buried the horrible "charm" confiscated from Jacky and the aboriginal bewailed his loss unavailingly.

A strange friendship sprung up between the black-tracker and Esther Pennycuick whose sex was never suspected by the Commissioner or any of the police. Indeed they saw very little of her during the next few weeks for she spent most of her time working with silent old Malachi on the claim. Esther Pennycuick hardly ever spoke to anyone except to Jacky. Even the jovial young Scotsman, Malcolm M'Lachlan, was almost ignored and began to talk of seeking other partners.

But the taciturn "boy", and the black-tracker from the police camp were constantly in close colloquy. If M'Lachlan had been in the least suspicious by temperament he would certainly have conjectured that a plot of some sort was brewing.

A NATIVE TRACKER.

1 3

Setting a Big Trap

"FATHER," said Esther Pennycuick one morning soon after the black-tracker's leg was quite strong again. "I'm going away for a few days to Bathurst. I want a rest very badly."

And indeed the girl looked as if she needed a holiday.

She was pale and thin, and terribly run down.

"All right," growled old Malachi. "Don't stay away long for I'll he lonely wi'out you, me girl." Malachi had become nervous and fretful of late as well as silent. Moreover, he had begun to talk in his sleep, and the fact worried him. He never spoke to Esther of David Venn, but he looked at her with a searching questioning faze at times, and whenever he did so Esther grew paler and more ill at ease than she was before.

So old Malachi got in two new chums to help him work the claim along with Malcolm M'Lachlan, and Esther rose at dawn, hid her revolver in the bosom of her Crimean shirt, and stole out of the camp down to the river where Jacky the black-tracker was waiting for her with a broad grin on his face and a sugar-bag full of rough tucker in his hand.

Esther Pennycuick knew that her heart would break if she stayed any longer on the diggings. She determine to find David Venn wherever he was hiding, and to join him in his mountain solitude. Therefore she had held many conferences with the black-tracker and Jacky had assured her that he could find the "white pfeller" no matter how closely he had hidden himself. Had not he, Jacky, already tracked David Venn all the way to Ponto Island in the Macquarie River and assisted in the capture which was effected by Trooper Mitford. He could do the same again - so he vigourously asserted with a liberal display of shining white teeth. White Mary might put her entire trust in him.

And, White Mary did.

They travelled on foot over the first part of the trail that Jacky had already hunted, and when they came to the Red Cobber's hut, hidden away behind its rampart of loose rocks, Jacky grasped the tomahawk that he carried in his belt, and clenched his teeth, while he walked warily, realising his danger to the full.

But, to his great relief, the Red Cobber was not here. However, the Red Cobber's footmarks were there and in the wide and uneven circles that they made the aboriginal could read the white man's clumsy efforts to find his vanished assailant. The footmarks were those of a man who staggered in an agony of suffering. But it could not subdue his yearning for revenge.

And then, with savage Intuition, Jacky read the intention of the Red Cobber in the footmarks that bore away from the plateau where the hut stood, and led down the long, grassy vista, towards the upward track that intersected it a few miles farther on from the Turon.

The Red Cobber was a friend of the man whom Trooper Mitford had been hunting - the strange man who escaped with David Venn from the bullock-chain. The Red Cobber had assisted that friend by rolling down rocks on Trooper Mitford's party, and by pretending that he was unable to speak when the trooper questioned him. Therefore, the Red Cobber, in his own emergency, would seek and follow the man whom he had befriended and who was the most likely person to befriend him in turn. All this was felt rather than consciously reasoned out by Jacky. It represented the course of events which was inevitable to a person actuated by the ordinary feelings of primitive human nature. And in guessing that the Red Cobber in his terrible mutilated state would follow the man who had evidently constituted himself guide to David Venn, the aboriginal at once grasped the bearing of this discovery upon his own problem.

All that he had to do was to follow the Red Cobber's footprints. Those footprints would lead him and White Mary to David Venn. And it was David Venn whom White Mary particularly desired to meet. Trooper Mitford and Jimmy had been led astray because they followed the hoofmarks of horses, and the same horses did not always carry the same riders. But he, Jacky, would track his enemy the Red Cobber by marks that could not be misleading. And his enemy would lead him to David Venn.

Jacky explained the situation roughly to Esther as she sat upon a log eating some bread and meat in order to get strength for the journey.

"Red Cobber him track white pfeller's mate. Jacky track Red Cobber. All ri.' Bimeby we findem white pfeller pretty soon, my word.'

The aboriginal made a close inspection of the marks made by the Red Cobber's great splay feet, and thus gave himself assurance that he could pick out those particular foot-marks from any others in the world. So when Esther had eaten her food, and Jacky had gnawed a mutton bone, they resumed their march along the grassy avenue that led downwards towards the track that rose from the river to join it. The tracks were, many days old, but the heavy rain that had put an end to Jimmy's task at Jessie's Corner fell before the Red Cobber, in his misery, began his journey towards his bushranging protector. There had been no rain since then, and consequently the Red Cobber's footprints were as legible as signposts. Indeed, to Jacky, they were infinitely more legible. He walked along, limping slightly on his left leg, and continually reassuring Esther that she would see David Venn" bimeby, plenty soon."

"Boys," cried Jack Dunphy to the group of card-players in the house in the tunnel. "I'm fair sick of doin' nothin'. Reckon they've forgotten about that fat old bishop an' his collection-money by this time, and, anyhow, I'm tired of stopping here. I'm for the road again."

"Right y'are," said Tom Warburton stifling a yawn.

"It's about time we made a move. What with the diggings in full blast at Hill End and Sofala, 'I'arnbaroora and Wattle Flat, there must be enough stuff comin' along the Bathurst road every day to make a man rich for life."

"That's just what I've been thinkin'," said Jaek Dunphy, "an' I'm out for it."

"So am I," said Tom Warburton.

"Me too," muttered Bill Rogers.

"I'll be there," said Charles Russell Fitzroy Stanhope languidly.

"What about you, Darby?"

The Red Cobber nodded his head vigorously. He yearned for action.

"And you, Venn ?"

David had already made up his mind that there was no going backward for him now. "I'm with you, of course," he said briefly. He hated the idea of robbing any person. He shrank from crime. But the security of Esther depended on his retaining the confidence of these desperate associates, for without their aid he would certainly be recaptured. So again his generous heart and his pure motive of self-sacrifice drove him forward along the dark and gloomy path of which he could by no means foresee the end. He was steeled to desperate deeds, not by a craving for crime, but by love for Esther Pennycuick.

Jack Dunphy unfolded his plan, which was of marvellous simplicity. He had had enough of isolated pettifogging robberies. He desired to carry out a big, comprehensive job. What was the use of sticking up a single horseman, or even a single mail coach, when it was just as easy to stick up the whole road?

Bill Rogers and Tom Warburton gazed at him open-mouthed. The beams of light that stole into the tunnel from the chinks in the interwoven foliage that formed the roof far above, and from both ends of the narrow gorge, where the bushwood that masked the entrances was thin, revealed Dunphy square-jawed, powerful, and resolute, sitting on an empty wooden case, expounding the points by waving his pipe which he held between his thumb and forefinger.

"All these diggers have plenty of the dust on them;' remarked Mr. Dunphy, with an assured air, "an' besides, there's the bullock drays comin' along regularly with big loads of stores that we need badly. There are rich Englishmen, too, an' tourists, an' officers, an' if we've any luck at all, we might even bag a couple of squatters or a police-inspector, and bail 'em up with everybody else."

"A regular picnic, by jove," ejaculated Mr. Stanhope. " Not a bad idea," exclaimed Dunphy quickly. "We'll make it a picnic - after the solid business part is finished, of course. I feel that I could do with a bit of pleasure, and, perhaps, even find a woman to talk to for a while. You chaps are all right, of course, but you ain't particularly amusing. Are you Bill?"

Bill Rogers scowled and puffed away at his pipe. "Don't you go a-throwin' off at me, cap," he grunted, sullenly, "'cause I wan't stand for it."

"All right Bill," said Dunphy, good-humouredly.

"You're a better horseman than conversationalist, so I'll give you a job at once. Take your horse, and get away as fast as you can to Jessie's Corner. See Ironbark Joe, and find out from him whether all the police are down at the Turon or whether there is any big body of them up this way. Bring back your report this afternoon, an' if everything is clear, we'll hold up the road to-night by Bottlebrush Flat."

"Jolly good fun, too," said Stanhope. "By gad Dunphy, I don't know how you come to think of these things - I don't really, by gad."

Dunphy looked at him out of the corner of his eye.

"The things that you don't know, Stanhope," he said, "'ud fill a dictionary. I ain't at all sure that you know even your own name. Reckon it ain't Stanhope, at any rate."

Stanhope gave a sickly grin, and pulled his long golden moustache. There were times when he did his best to forget his own name, and now this coarse brute was sticking a knife into his heart with his horrible hints. He subsided into silence.

And then Dunphy proceeded to explain his idea at greater length. He proposed to bar the main road leading to Bathurst at a convenient position near Bottlebrush Flat where there was a large cleared space in the bush suitable for his purpose. Every person who came along the road, whether man, woman, or child, would be impounded without any distinction and compelled to go to the cleared space in the bush which was only a few hundred yards from the road-just far enough, in fact, to enable those who had already been caught to be hidden from the sight of unsuspecting next comers. Bullock-drays and other vehicles would also be withdrawn into the bush. The bushrangers would take possession of all money and valuables and of such stores as they required. With proper care the contingency of any person escaping to warn the police could be guarded against. A camp would be formed in the cleared space and the captives might be kept there until the continually-increasing number grew too large to be accommodated in the space available or until word was received from the scouts that danger was approaching. In that event the members of the gang would disappear with all speed and would meet again at Mount Elephant - in the tunnel. If by any mischance the police should get near enough to follow any of them and thus discover the entrance to the tunnel there was a free exit at the other end, and every man would have to secure his own safety by whatever means he thought best.

This explanation was not given in the form of a continuous narrative, but as answers to innumerable questions which were fired at their inventive leader by every member of the gang in succession. The Red Cobber, among the others, listened eagerly, but, alas, he was not able to express his opinions on it. His face, however, plainly indicated a slight trace of disappointment.

"You don't see much fun in it 'cause there isn't to be any fighting. That's it, isn't it, Darby?"

The Red Cobber nodded his head eagerly.

"Well, something might happen before the picnic is over," said Dunphy, with a laugh. "It's impossible to say always how a little matter like this will turn out."

The Red Cobber brightened up wonderfully. The prospect of doing some damage to anybody - no matter who it might be - seemed to cheer him up remarkably.

In the afternoon Bill Rogers returned from his scouting expedition with cheering news. Ironbark Joe had narrated to him the arrival of the enraged bishop at the Honeymoon Inn, and close on his heels the appearance of two troopers and a black tracker. The innkeeper further related for the information of Dunphy how he had personally lamed the horses of the troopers, so as to make further pursuit impossible, and mentioned that they had gone back to the Turon next day, and that the bishop had departed for Bathurst *en route* for Sydney, threatening to have a regiment of soldiers sent up to restore order and security on the goldfields area. Ironbark Joe congratulated Dunphy on the success of his ruse in exchanging horses with the bishop, and reported that there were no police nearer than the Turon. He also reported that travellers were numerous and cash plentiful.

Even the humorless Bill Rogers made his companions laugh heartily when he passed on to them Ironbark Joe's description of the discom-

discomfiture of Mitford and Mahoney when they realised that they had caught a bishop in mistake for a bushranger.

Bill even ventured to imitate Ironbark Joe himself in his conversation with the bishop;-

"So I says, says I, 'Surely they must be terrible villains,' says I, 'to attack yer Excellency,' says I, 'and the roads are getting so unsafe these days,' says I, 'that the Pope himself,' says I, 'saving the presence of' yer Imminence, wouldn't be free from the blaggards - no, he wudn't.' An' then the bishop said he was glad to meet an honest man, an' he axed me to partake of a little light refreshment with him, so I brought out a drop of real 'moonshine' that I made in my own still and we made a night of it. His lordship told me just before he rode away in the morning that he never tasted a better drop of stuff in his life, an' he axed me where I bought it, but I never told him about the pot still an' th' quinces."

"The quinces," said Dunphy, in puzzled tones. "Why quinces?"

And so Bill Rogers let his leader into a little secret well known to the moonshiners all through the mountains from the Hawkesbury to the Macquarie, namely that the best whisky is made from those big yellow quinces that grow so prolifically and can be treated in the still so conveniently.

Bill Rogers went on to say that Ironbark Joe had received word from a trusted source that old Montgomery, the owner of the run upon which Darby Kennedy had been employed as shepherd, had been up north, and was returning to Bathurst on the following day. He was travelling on horseback unattended, and would probably he carrying a considerable sum with him in cash.

The Red Cobber, who was listening with the closest attention to Bill's recital, grinned in a ghastly fashion at this item of intelligence. 'He had no love for old Montgomery, who was accustomed to pay him skinflint wages, and to make disagreeable enquiries about the steady disappearance of the sheep reported to him by his manager as missing while under Kennedy's care. If old Montgomery walked, or rather rode, into the snare at Bottlebrush Flat it would be an excellent opportunity, in the Red Cobber's opinion, for the repayment of old scores.

Exhilarated at the prospect of action and excitement after a period of enforced inactivity, the men ate a hearty meal - provisions of the best were stored in plenty in the tunnel - and then had a short sleep so as to be ready for the work of the night. There was a good deal of scouting to be done, and also some slight preparations were necessary at the scene of the projected hold-up and temporary encampment.

At nightfall Jack Dunphy collected his forces, and the men and their horses left the tunnel by the eastern exit. They slid and scrambled down into the valley, where Jack Dunphy made his final dispositions. Stanhope and Tom Warburton were to go north and south respectively, keeping wide of the main road, and calling for information at the huts of various persons with whom they were well acquainted, and who would be able to tell them if the police made any move at the eleventh hour unknown to Ironbark Joe. They were also to find out what travellers of importance might be expected along the road on the following day. If either of them became aware of a move on the part of the police or of any other unforseen danger he was to gallop at once to Bottlebrush Flat with the warning.

Stanhope and Tom Warburton disappeared into the night, and the remainder, consisting of Dunphy, Bill Rogers, the Red Cobber, and David Venn, moved off slowly to strike the main road at Bottlebrush Flat, five miles away.

As they rode away in single file across the creek and through the saplings and light timber that clothed the valley, the gigantic outline of Mount Elephant towered up behind them. Keeping an easterly course, they had the rising moon in front of them, and climbing over a saddle in the second range that closed in the valley opposite to Mount Elephant, they walked their horses carefully over the loose boulders and entered more open country at last. No gold diggers had penetrated as far as this. The land was still in its primeval condition. Progress was slow, but Dunphy was the guide, and he made no mistake. After riding for a couple of hours, the four men came out on the white road shining in the moonlight and curving away into the distance. Not a soul was in sight, and not a sound was to be heard, except the tapping of their own horses' hoofs on the hard surface.

But Dunphy had no intention of exposing either himself or the men who accepted his leadership unnecessarily. He motioned them back into the bush that fringed the road, and they continued to force their way through the saplings for another half-mile, when a halt was called. It was a splendid natural position for the proposed exploit. No trained strategist could have selected a better one. Coming up from south to north, the road at the spot picked out by Dunphy bent sharply to the east, then swung to the west, avoiding the high, impracticable, rocky ground straight ahead, and almost immediately straightened and resumed its northerly direction. The sharp double bend resembled an indentation or nick so formed that the road made a kind of pocket shut in on each side by high, rocky ground. Through this pocket, traffic from both north and south had to pass, nor was it possible to see what was happening within the 'curve unbil one had turned the corner either from the north or from the south. It was a regular mousetrap, easy enough to get into from either side, but impossible to get out of, especially when he roadway was obstructed by a substantial barrier and both the northern and southern exits were. held by armed men.

The road was fringed with heavy timber and a big blue-gum rose gaunt and grey on the edge of the curve.

Dunphy, who forgot nothing, produced an axe, and handed it to David Venn. "There's your job," he said.

pointing to the big blue-gum. "You've got to get him down somehow."

David Venn was a clever axeman, but the sweat was rolling off him before he had cut half way through the tough trunk. So Bill Rogers took the axe for a spell, and the steady thud-thud of the steel head upon the blue-gum sounded far through the quiet night.

"Take a turn at it, Darby," said Dunphy, when Bill Rogers began to flag, and the Red Cobber, seizing the axe, put in some mighty upward and downward strokes on the side of the tree facing towards the road.

"Look out, boys, here she comes." There was a rush for cover as the blue-gum toppled over with a mighty crash, lying right across the highway, and interposing a barricade of three feet of solid timber to all traffic.

14

The Trap Closes

OUTSIDE the curve the rocky formation on both sides of the road came to an end, and on the west side, approaching the pocket from the south, a practicable track led into the heart of the bush. A quarter of a mile up this track the ground opened out into a grassy plain, dotted here and there with bottlebrush. This was Bottlebrush Flat. There were signs that somebody had once tried to do a bit of clearing and to build a hut there, but the adventurous settler, whoever he was, had wearied of the laborious task, and the place was quickly going back to its primeval aspect.

Dunphy rode through the bush to the open space, and surveyed it with approval. "Just the place for a picnic, ain't it?" he said to David, with a grin, and David was obliged to admit that the place seemed made for the purpose.

Returning to the road and to the barricade, which was completely hidden from travellers approaching either from the north or the south by reason of the sharp entering and. leaving curves, Dunphy and Venn found that the scouts had arrived.

It was now long after midnight, and Stanhope and Warburton had covered a good deal of country. Their horses were leg-weary and covered with foam. They reported no, signs of police. Several loaded bullock drays had been made out, the bullocks grazing in the bush, and the bullock drivers camping by their fires. Tom Warburton had travelled nearly as far as Mudgee, and Stanhope had been down to Capertee Valley. They had seen many camp-fires in both directions, and they reckoned that there would be great business doing at Bottlebrush Flat next day.

"And, Dunphy, don't forget that the mail coach from the Castlereagh will pass through to-morrow afternoon."

But Dunphy had not forgotten. Indeed, he seemed to forget nothing. He even remembered that the men might as well have some food and a couple of hours' sleep before daybreak as there would be nothing doing until then.

Having made all his preparations the leader of the bushrangers lighted his pipe and contemplated the blue-gum barrier across the road with quiet satisfaction. Everything was ready. Scouts were out on both sides, for Stanhope and Warburton had given the office to certain settlers and bush publicans, who supervised all passers-by on the road, and horses were held in readiness, so that in the event of the police putting in an appearance, timely warning could be given to the men holding Bottlebrush Flat.

Soon after dawn a faint rumble could be heard on the road to the south.

"Bullock-dray comin' up from Bathurst," reported Warburton, who had been out scouting and returned through the bush unseen by the bullock-driver.

The rumbling grew louder, and presently the lurid remarks addressed by the bullocky to his animals and the loud cracks of his terrible whip broke upon the expectant ears of Iack Dunphy. "Out of sight, all of you," said the leader, and the men hastily took up their positions.

Lying down behind the blue-gum barrier were Stanhope, Warburton, and Rogers, with pistols loaded. Dunphy, Venn, and the Red Cobber took cover just behind the angle of the rock round which the road curved sharply into the pocket

The huge, lumbering dray was drawn by nine pairs of bullocks, which moved along at a speed of about two miles an hour, the leading pair being ever so far away from Bullocky Ned, who walked beside the polers, shouting words of encouragement. or abuse at intervals as the nature of the road demanded.

So it happened that the leading bullocks disappeared round the curve of the road while Bullocky Ned ruminated on his past sins and contemplated fresh ones. All at once the team came to a dead standstill.

"Geddup, Smoker! Geddup, Baldy!" yelled Ned Butt, cracking the long whip in a succession of loud reports, but not a move could be got out of the sapient bullocks.

Ned Butt went forward to investigate. The obstacle that could stop his bullocks must indeed be a formidable one. As he strode round the corner he caught sight of the huge tree lying right across the road, and the leading pair of bullocks standing stolidly within a foot of it. They could go through or over most obstructions, but they were wise bullocks, and they knew their own limitations. They were not tree-climbers.

As Bullocky Ned stepped up to the fallen log to investigate it, three men, with their faces concealed with black crepe, rose up from behind it, and each of them held a pistol. Ned Butt turned round to run back to the dray, which was still outside the curve. He found his escape cut off by three more men, also in black masks and carrying firearms.

"Hands up, Ned," said Dunphy, who had apparently met the bullocky before, "you're fairly caught."

Ned's vocabulary was naturally fluent and vigorous. It had been brought to perfection by constant association with his team, which worked with super-bovine energy when Ned uncorked his full flow of vigorous profanity. But he was speechless in the presence of this overpowering calamity, which had come upon him with the swiftness and unexpectedness of a thunderbolt. "Well, I'll be --" he muttered, and there he stuck. He held up his hands, and Dunphy went through his pockets, extracting nothing therefrom except 'a battered half-crown, a knife, a plug of tobacco, a very odoriferous pipe, and a box of wax matches. These articles were at once handed back to the owner.

But, meanwhile willing hands had explored the dray, which was loaded with stores of all descriptions, consigned to the northern diggings. A substantial sum in gold coin was unearthed from the bottom of a box of canned meats, where it was hidden in a leather bag, for Bullocky Ned was a trader on his own account as well as a carrier, and he took his capital with him. He found his voice at last when he saw the money being emptied into Dunphy's capacious pocket, and his language would have lifted his team out of the worst bog between

Tambaroora and Boggabri.

"Hold yer jaw, Ned," said Dunphy softly, "or I'll fix ye so that ye'll have to. Come here, Darby, and show our new friend what happened to you."

The Red Cobber came forward, huge, menacing, silent.

Obediently, but with a horrible grin, he opened his cavernous mouth, and cold sweat trickled down Ned Butt's back when he saw that the giant had no tongue. Ned at once concluded that the terrible punishment had been inflicted by the leader of the gang. Thenceforward, in trembling horror of unknown atrocious penalties, he obeyed Dunphy with precipitancy, and displayed the same instant obedience to the commands of every member of the gang. Ned Butt had had his lesson. The Red Cobber was a living warning.

It happened that David Venn was selected to keep guard over Bullocky Ned while, in obedience to Dunphy's order, he conducted the bullock-dray up the track through the bush and into the cleared open space beyond. David undertook this duty stolidly. After all, it was for Esther's sake. He comforted himself with that thought.

"Kin I have a drop o' rum off the dray?" enquired Bullocky Ned, humbly, " Me teeth is chatterin'."

The required consent was given, but David declined to drink himself, and Ned Butt tossed off a stiff pannikin of rum and water alone.

"'Ow long am I goin' to be kep' 'ere?" inquired the bullocky. David did not know, but he thought that the bullocks might be unyoked and allowed to graze. There was no likelihood of their being required to resume the journey immediately.

So Ned proceeded to unyoke his bullocks, and when he found himself engaged in that familiar task he actually began to whistle, and presently, realising the wisdom of making the best of the situation, be became quite friendly. By David's permission he lit a fire and put the billy on to make tea.

As Ned Butt waited for the billy to boil the first of a whole series of involuntary visitors arrived. It was old Montgomery, the squatter, spluttering with indignation at the outrageous manner in which he had been robbed of every penny in his pocket and also deprived of his fine, upstanding, nearly thorough-bred roadster. The Red Cobber his former employee, propelled him roughly along the track, gripping the little, spare, parchment-visaged old man by the collar with unnecessary violence.

The Red Cobber had never felt his loss of the power of speech so bitterly as when he was face to face at last with the parismonious old man who had periodically docked his wages on account of the missing sheep that the shepherd was unable to account for. But though Darby had no tongue with. which to lash his former employer, he still had a pair of very large and serviceable feet, and whenever old Montgomery stopped to expostulate, Darby Kennedy kicked him violently in the region best adapted to receive the toe of a boot.

The old man was almost beside himself with pain and rage when he reached the clearing, but as soon as the Red Cobber had gone back to the road the squatter adapted himself perforce to his surroundings, and, sitting down on a log, drank the pannikin of tea that Bullocky Ned poured out for him, and devoured thankfully enough the bread and meat that were brought from the dray.

David Venn had two prisoners to look after now. But they gave him no trouble at all, and escape was obviously impossible.

Meanwhile business was booming at the barricade. Mr. Harold St. John and Mr. Arthur Ponsonby, two wealthy young Englishmen who were seeing the world together, arrived on: horseback, attended by Jim Bates, their English body-servant, and were promptly impounded. They carried off the misadventure with a hearty laugh, for they had only a few sovereigns in their pockets. They were' escorted to the clearing by Tom Warburton, who remained there with them, as the prisoners were now getting too numerous for David Venn to supervise single-handed. Mr. St. John and Mr. Ponsonby fraternised with old Montgomery, while Jim Bates set to work to provide them with breakfast, Bullocky Ned surveying him all the time with quiet amusement. As the morning wore on, new visitors began to arrive at the clearing in considerable numbers. They all behaved in much the same way. At first they were angry and frightened, but when they saw their companions in misfortune making the best of it, they cheered up, and found each other's experiences an inexhaustible topic of discussion. There were several gold-seekers on their way to the Turon in carts or on foot.

One of them was propelling a wheelbarrow containing all his worldly goods, when he ran right into the fallen gum-tree and the levelled pistols behind it.

A few settlers going down for a trip to Bathurst had their wives and children with them. The kiddies regarded the picnic in the bush as the best of fun, and raced about, shrieking with glee, and making friends with everybody.

Dunphy allowed no one to pass through in either direction. Rich or poor, whether they could contribute much or nothing to the ever-increasing pile of loot, they all had to join the assemblage at the clearing. None could be permitted to leave the place lest warning of what was happening might be conveyed to the police.

In the afternoon the mail coach from the north came swinging along, and its progress was duly arrested by the impassable barrier. George Belton, the driver, and his six passengers were levied upon for their portable property, and the mail bags were ripped open and the registered packages opened. Then Belton and his passengers were conducted to the clearing, where, to their great astonishment, they found more than fifty people assembled.

Mr. St. John and Mr. Ponsonby had organised races for the children, with prizes of bottles of lollies obtained from the bullock-dray. Ned Butt produced a concertina, and sitting on the edge of his dray, discoursed dance music; which Mr. St. John and Mr. Ponsonby did not disdain to utilise, taking as their partners the two daughters of a local settler, who had been impounded with the rest. After the dance, a saturnine individual, who was believed to be a university professor in the rough habiliments of a gold-digger, obliged with a song. The bacchanalian strains of "The Little Brown Jug" sounded far and wide from Bottlebrush Flat, and floated away into the distant ranges.

15

A Surprise Attack

IT was while Esther Pennycuick, in her Crimean shirt and moleskins, was climbing down the stoniest of a whole succession of stony ranges that the faint strains of "The Little Brown Jug" smote upon her ears. Jacky heard the sound, too, and listened intently..

"Big mob white pfellers, my word," said Jacky in perplexity. "Plenty yabber-yabber."

Jacky intimated that it would be wise to investigate this unusual phenomenon. He had lost the Red Cobber's tracks hopelessly, but had picked up other tracks, which seemed to him to be well worth following- the tracks of no fewer than six horses. Closely followed by Esther, he crept through the light scrub till he reached the edge of the clearing. Peering through the saplings he signalled to Esther, whose gaze followed Jacky's pointing finger.

The scene that she saw riveted her with amazement ¬the bullocks unyoked from the dray grazing on the fiat, the bullock-driver playing the concertina with unfeigned enjoyment, several couples footing it neatly on the green, men and women sitting on the ground, laughing, chatting, eating, and drinking, a horde of children racing about, shrieking joyously - and, standing apart from the picnickers, absorbed in thought, the figure of David Venn!

With difficulty Esther repressed her impulse to cry out.

A warning hiss from Jacky made her keep silence. Then Jacky pointed to David Venn. "White Mary's man," he muttered. "White Mary all ri' now. Jacky gettem back bimeby soon; sit down alonga Turon." He vanished like a black snake through the bush, and Esther found herself alone.

"David!" What was that voice that came to him through the confused hum of the motley throng around him. David Venn thought for one horrible instant that his brain was going. His gloomy pondering over the. strange course of events that had made him the associate of outlaws must have shaken his nerves to pieces.

"David!" The voice rang out more loudly the second time. Startled and anxious, recognising the voice at once, but fearing that the sound had no existence to any ear save his own, David Venn looked across the clearing, and there, emerging from the saplings, he saw the boyish little figure he knew so well. His knees trembled under him, for he was sure that what he saw was an hallucination. How could Esther possibly have got there? Yet he found himself running towards the vision.

Tom Warburton, the other guard, had gone back to the road. The picnickers were too busily engaged to pay attention to the movements of their solitary gaoler, and when David Venn walked up to Esther and took her hand he was unnoticed by his prisoners.

"David, David, I could not stay at the Turon without you," said Esther, with the tears in her voice. "So I got Jacky, the black-tracker, to bring me to you. But now I am quite mystified. Won't you tell me what you are doing here?"

"I am a bushranger," said David, bitterly, "a bushranger against my will"- and he told her the identity of the drunken man whom she had helped to escape from the bullock-chain. Yes, it was quite true. That man was the notorious Jack Dunphy, and had it not been for his assistance - he, David, would certainly have been recaptured.

Esther turned white as a sudden thought flashed into her mind. "And you have done all this for me," she whispered. "You have made yourself an outlaw to save me from being taken by the police for shooting Morosini, and to protect me from the discovery that I am a woman. Oh, David, David, I can't bear it!"

They were some distance away from the picnickers.

And Esther cried.

"You mustn't cry, dear," said David. " They will see you. You must come back to the camp with me. In all that big muster

Across the clearing he saw the boyish little figure he knew so well.

nobody will know that you are not one of themselves. And then when they are released, as they will be to-night, why Dunphy and all of us go away, you, can go with them and return to your father at the Turon."

"I cannot go back to my father, I cannot, I cannot," sobbed Esther, her whole body shaking with emotion.

"But surely the old man will need you," said David, somewhat puzzled at this new turn of events.

"I cannot help it," said Esther, looking at David appealingly. "I will never go back to live with my father again. I want to stay with you always."

David was more puzzled than ever. He had escaped with Dunphy in order to save Esther from the police, and enable her to live on quietly with her father at Golden Point. Yet now she wanted to share his outlawry.

"Hullo! How did your mate get here, Venn?" David was startled from his reverie, and looking behind him, saw Dunphy on the bishop's horse, surveying Esther with astonishment.

"He followed us, up," said David, hurriedly. "He wants to come along and join me. I was just trying to persuade him to go back to the Turon."

"Well, you're a likely-looking lad," said Dunphy to Esther Pennycuick, an' if it hadn't been for the file you brought us I reckon I might have been anchored to that bullock-chain still. If you want to join us you can."

So that is how Fate stretched out a hand, plucked up Esther Pennycuick from her life of honorable toil at the Turon diggings, and transplanted her into the lawless and desperate environment from which David Venn, who loved her, was fiercely yearning to escape.

As Dunphy was still talking to David Venn, the two men noticed a sudden commotion among the picnickers who were impounded in the clearing. '" They were startled immediately by a loud cheer."

"By the Lord," cried Dunphy, "they're going to break out," and, cocking his pistol, he galloped off."Back there, you dogs! " he yelled. "Get back or I'll drop a few of you in the tracks!"

But the captives only cheered all the more loudly.

"Ha! you scoundrels" it was the thin, cracked falsetto of old Montgomery, screaming shrilly - "you'll get your deserts at last. The gallows for everyone of you."

Dunphy fired at the old man, who was running as fast as he could for the road, and missed him.

At the same instant another shot rang out and a bullet passed through the bushrangers hat.

"Look out, men," he yelled, "the troopers are all round us!"

It was only too true. Mr. Commissioner Grey had given up employing half measures. He had sent down to Sydney for reinforcements to deal with Dunphy's gang, and twenty troopers, under sub-inspector Tallard, had been sent up to him. The sub-inspector was smart and experienced. One of Dunphy's "bush telegraphs" had blowed the gaff for a consideration, and when the whole business was going like a party Tallard and his man rode through the bush and drew a cordon round Bottlebrush Flat.

Events moved rapidly in the next half-minute. There was a brisk fusillade of pistol shots, a confused sound of cheering and cursing, and then Esther realised that she was mounted behind David Venn, and 'that they were charging the police cordon just behind Dunphy.

David knew that to be captured meant imprisonment for life, at the very least, for him, as he was certain to be convicted of the killing of Morosini, though the verdict might be reduced from murder to manslaughter. He knew also that Esther's sex would be discovered if she were arrested, and complicity in the murder probably suspected. He touched his horse with the spur and raced after Dunphy.

Behind them was a din of shouts, curses, and pistol shots, as Stanhope and Warburton, Rogers and the Red Cobber, burst through the crowd of captives and galloped towards various points of the encircling cordon.

Stanhope was the first to fall. A trooper's bullet went through his shoulder, and he tumbled from the saddle into a patch of brushwood. As he lay there, Mr. Arthur Ponsonby ran up to him and gazed intently at his features. "By the lord," he ejaculated, "it's Delville of St. Ambrose's, all right - the chap that was caught with three aces in his pocket in Filstead's rooms. You remember him, Harold."

Yes, Mr. St. John remembered him quite well, and helped the trooper, who had shot him, to staunch the bleeding.

Warburton and Rogers were overpowered after firing their pistols unavailingly, but the Red Cobber, who had seized old Montgomery's horse, a magnificent bay thorough-bred, dashed through the ring of armed men, escaping their bullets by a miracle, and vanished into the light timber.

It was well for Dunphy and David Venn that they were riding the bishop's clean-bred pair.

The police who had surrounded the curious encampment at Bottlebrush Flat were drawing their cordon more tightly round the centre of the camp when their presence was discovered by one of the captives, and the premature cheering put Dunphy on the *qui vive*, and gave him a chance that he was quick to see. The troopers were separated from each other by wide intervals at first, and the only chance of escape was to get through the cordon before the intervals closed up as the men advanced.

Dunphy's mount stood seventeen hands high, a weight carrier up to twenty stone, and of great bone and substance. He had been used principally in the saddle, and with a resolute rider on his back, he was a fine goer, with plenty of courage.

David Venn's horse was almost a facsimile of the other, for the pair had been matched with fastidious care. As David felt Esther's arms around him, he was absolutely thrilled. It would take a strong man to stop such a rider on such a horse by any other means than a bullet through the heart.

Trooper Beggs, one of the reinforcing detachment from Sydney, looked up and saw a big man on a big brown horse, and another big brown horse carrying double. The two horses were charging straight for the cordon at the point occupied by Trooper Mahoney, who was about seventy yards from Beggs.

"Look out, Mahoney," yelled Beggs. "Use the carbine man. Stop 'em, stop 'em. Oh, Lord! "

He could see Mahoney's red face quite distinctly.

Mahoney was riding a great raw-boned, lop-eared, white horse, with a head as big as a portmanteau. What on earth was the fellow doing with his carbine. Trooper Beggs became aware that Mahoney had dropped the percussion cap from the nipple of his carbine, and was fumb¬ling with another cap, which he was trying to place in position.

Trooper Beggs put his own carbine to his shoulder and fired at Dunphy, but the bullet went wide. He might as well have tried to hit a pigeon on the wing with a rifle ball at seventy yards.

Ah! Mahoney had fixed the percussion cap at last, and wa; raising his carbine to his shoulder. The man on the big brown horse was evidently unarmed, for he displayed no weapon of any kind, not even a stick. It was any odds that he would surrender when he saw the barrel of the carbine in front of him. These were the thoughts that flashed through the mind of Trooper Beggs.

But the fellow showed no sign of stopping.

"Surrender now, or I'll let the daylight t'roo ye! "

The words rang out in Mahoney's mighty voice, and Trooper Beggs heard them distinctly. As they were uttered, it came into the mind of Beggs that the man on the big brown horse was not going to surrender, in spite of the loaded carbine in Mahoney's hand. Trooper Beggs touched his horse with the spur to go to Mahoney's assistance.

But before he had well started, something happened that was quite unexpected.

The man on the big brown horse bent his head down almost to the horse's withers, and rode at racing pace straight at Trooper Mahoney, who had pulled his own horse round till he stood at right angles to the line taken by the charging bushranger.

Trooper Beggs held his breath, and his eyes were opened to their widest.

A fraction of a second before the collision Dunphy swung the big brown horse to the left without checking his terrific pace in the slightest. The great, powerful weight-carrier took the impact with his off shoulder, which struck the goose-rump of the trooper's lop-eared white horse a glancing blow, and toppled him over with a crash. For a second the brown horse. faltered, but Dunphy's powerful arms kept him on his feet, and he flew on with the speed of a railway train towards the ranges.

David Venn and Esther, on the second horse, had a clear run through the broken cordon, and a little cloud of dust rolling rapidly into the distance was all that Trooper Beggs could see of them as he pulled his horse up alongside the white horse on the ground with the motionless form of Mahoney beside him.

"No use trying to chase racehorses with this old crock," muttered Trooper Beggs, mournfully, "so I may as well have a look at Mahoney. Poor old chap, I expect he's done for."

Peggs slipped off his horse, and saw at once that the old white troop-horse had his near hind-leg broken. The trooper pulled out his pistol, and a friendly bullet. ended the sufferings of the disabled animal. Then he turned his attention to Malioney, who was lying very still.

"Skull fractured, I suppose," said Beggs to himself, sorrowfully. "A blow like that would kill a bullock."

But as he was walking towards the figure lying prone on the ground, it moved, and then sat up it. Mahoney rubbed his eyes gently.

"Bedad ," he grumbled, "the dhurty felly wudn't wait till I got a shot at him. Shute, he was for all the wurruld like a cross between a wild bull and a locomotive, an' it's a bit av luck for me that he didn't shtrike me fair an' square, for, begob, I belave he might hav' hurted me if he had."

Still rubbing his head, Mahoney removed his saddle and accoutrements, and walked beside trooper Beggs, who led his horse back to the scene of the recent picnic encampment.

Scowling and silent, on a log sat Warburton and Rogers, handcuffed, with a trooper in front of them, carbine in hand. Delville, of St. Ambrose's, alias Charles Russell Stanhope, was lying in a rude litter with his right shoulder broken. Sub-inspector Tallard surveyed his prisoners thoughtfully.

"Got three out of the six, at any rate, Mitford," he said, "but the biggest fish have got away, I'm afraid. That red-headed fellow didn't give us much of a chance, but you made a nice muddle of your job with the other two, Mahoney."

The trooper looked very crestfallen. "Begob, sir, I t'ought I had 'em safe as rats in a trap, so I did, but the big felly on the brown harrse, he came at me like a cannonball, and the first thing I knew wuz bein' unconscious. Shure, I'm mortal sorry the t'ree of 'em got away."

"Two only," corrected the sub-inspector, " my information is that there were six of them altogether, and we have three of them here. The red-headed fellow got away on the other side, and then there were these two, who bowled you over and disappeared."

Mahoney scratched his head again. "Faix, there was t'ree of 'em wint pasht me annyway," he said, "an' two of 'em was ridin' on th' wan harrse."

"Oh, youv'e been seeing double," said the sub-inspector, testily, but Mahoney still stuck to his story, and refused to be corrected.

"T'ree of 'em," he muttered obstinately, "an' wan of 'em waz a bit avashlip av a boy no higher'n meshowlder."

So Mr. Tallard entered in his notebook that three men and a boy had made their escape. He had no doubt whatever in his mind that he could lay his hands on them within twenty-four hours if he liked, seeing that he had such a strong body of mounted men at his disposal. But he had a good deal of necessary routine work to do taking the names of all the persons who had been robbed, for instance, together with a list of the articles stolen and as it was already close on sunset, there was nothing to be gained by going after the fugitives at once.

So the miscellaneous gathering of travellers resumed their journeys that had been so rudely interrupted, and Mr. Tallard and his troopers, together with their prisoners, bivouacked on the deserted picnic ground, after the wounded man had been sent away in a spring cart, under a police escort, to the Bathurst Gaol infirmary.

But far away in the ranges Esther Pennycuick, in her boy's clothes, sat beside David Venn, in front of a log fire, which made weird reflections on the rock wall of the house in the tunnel. And Dunphy and the Red Cobber snored in their respective corners.

The girl shivered, and covered her face with her hands.

David Venn put his arm around her. He was terribly sorry for her. It was too tragic that such a young and innocent girl should have been driven by her fears to destroy the life of a fellow creature. He felt that, though he could take the guilt upon his own shoulders as far as the law was concerned, still he could not ease the burden of remorse that was lying on her conscience, it was the slaying of Morosini that made her so silent and pale and haggard.

"Do not be sad, dearest," he whispered in her ear, as they gazed into the red depths of the log fire. "By every law of God or man your deed was justified. Who knows what the Italian might have done if you had not reached for the gun and shot him!·'

But instead of being comforted, Esfher Pennycuick burst into tears.

1 6

A Bushranger's Incognito

IT was a curious existence that was led by the remnant of the gang in the house in the tunnel.

Dunphy was surly and morose for the first few days while they were lying hidden after the audacious exploit at Bottlebrush Flat. The Red Cobber disappeared from the retreat every morning regularly, but came back at night for food and shelter. He spent the day prowling round the mountains with a big sheath knife stuck in his belt, searching, always searching, for the black enemy who had stunned and mutilated him in his sleep. The quest became an obsession with him. He thought of nothing else in his waking hours. He dreamed of nothing else in the night hours, when the wind whistled down the two narrow valleys into which the tunnel opened east and west.

Jack Pennycuick - Esther was definitely Jack now, and it was imperative that the deception should be kept up - prepared the meals and kept the house in order while David Venn kept close guard over her. He noticed with much concern that the shooting of Morosini had seriously affected her. She was no longer the bright and joyous girl, whose gaiety had charmed him from the moment that he met her. Gloomy and taciturn, she went about her self-imposed tasks, as though seeking to distract her mind by hard, manual labour from thoughts of the tragic past.

At last, one morning Dunphy remarked that a man might as well be dead as be cooped up in that hole any longer. He proposed to ride into Bathurst, and, after making a few judicious alterations in his personal appearance, to attend the court and witness the trial of

Stanhope, Rogers, and Warburton. He took a melancholy pleasure in speculating upon their chances, and was quite unaware that Starihope had been wounded.

So Dunphy rode away on the bishop's horse, after carefully shaving off his stiff, black beard and leaving the whiskers, an operation that was not accomplished without great difficulty, He wore his customary attire, a pair of very dirty moleskin breeches, tucked into high boots, an old brown coat, full of holes, and a nondescript hat.

Next day the bishop's horse was pulled up in front of the Royal Hotel at Bathurst, and a fashionably-dressed gentleman alighted, wearing a suit of broadcloth, an expensive beaver, and a pair of Dundreary whiskers. It was Dunphy. The unfortunate original owner and wearer of the garments had been unlucky enough to meet the bushranger about twenty miles on the Bathurst side of Mount Elephant, and had been compelled to make an exchange of garments. Dressed in bushranger's weather-worn clothes, he went away lamenting, and also cursing. His name was Mr. Robert Pinkie, and he occupied a prominent position in Sydney society, being, in fact, a well-known banker, He wore a full black beard, and of him more anon.

When Dunphy extracted from the pocket of his well-cut, double-breasted waistcoat, a neat silver card case, and presented to the constable on duty at the door a visiting card ell graved in copperplate, with the very respectable legend, "Mr. Robert Pinkie, Evergreen Hall, Darling Point, Sydney," he was ushered at once into the court, where he modestly found a seat at the back, next to a rather wild-eyed, old gentleman, who had a very disagreeable habit of muttering to himself.

"Your servant, sir," said Dunphy, politely, to the old gentleman. "I think I have had the pleasure of seeing you at the Turon."

The old gentleman glared at him from under shaggy brows. "Woe unto them that are wise in their own eyes and prudent in their own sight," he rasped, "for, as the fire devoureth the stubble and the flame consumeth the chaff, so their root shall be as rottenness, and their blossom shall go up as dust."

"Ah," said Dunphy, politely, for the judge had not yet taken his seat on the bench, and the hum of conversation was general, "and may I ask, sir, whether you have any special interest in the case of the unhappy men who are shortly to be tried for an audacious violation of the public peace?"

"I am brought here to give testimony, if need be," rumbled the old gentleman, "and behold, I will arise and scatter mine enemies, for the child of my old age is departed, and my house is left unto me desolate." The old gentleman began to discharge a perfect battery of texts, and Dunphy's desire for conversation was speedily appeased. "Rats in the garret," muttered Dunphy to himself, " and religious rats, too - the most dangerous kind of all." He settled himself clown to listen to the trial of Warburton and Rogers, who stood in the dock behind a formidable row of iron spikes, and with a warder on each side of them.

Council for the Crown opened the case against the prisoners, calmly and dispassionately describing the audacious manner in which they had assisted to bail up every person travelling on the main highway, and narrating with much detail how they had been captured by the well-laid plans of that very energetic officer, Sub-inspector Tallard,

The day was hot, and the witnesses droned along, forging an unbreakable chain of evidence against the prisoners in the dock. Dunphy's head nodded forward on his breast. Suddenly he sat up, with everyone of his senses keenly on the alert.

"You say," council for the Crown was rapping out in harsh, incisive tones, "that these men in the dock were mere subordinates, who gave obedience to a much more dangerous criminal, their leader, and the planner of every robbery."

"That is so, sir," replied the witness. " And who was that leader?"

"A man of the name of Jack Dunphy," replied the Sub-inspector, "the most determined and resourceful criminal that I have ever come across. He escaped from custody at the Turon in the company of a man who had been arrested on a charge of murder. We have evidence that Dunphy and this other man, Venn, were both at Bottlebrush Flat, but, unfortunately, they escaped."

"Have you any doubt at all that the prisoners were associated with this man Dunphy?"

"None whatever, sir. We are in possession of admissions from both of them that they actually lived in Dunphy's hiding place. They resolutely refused to describe the situation of the hiding place, and so, also, did the third prisoner, who was wounded severely, and is still in the gaol hospital, but their refusal has not affected my plans."

"How is that?"

"I have ascertained the position of the hiding place from one of our black-trackers. It seems that he was following one of the gang, whom he calls the Red Cobber, and with whom he has some personal quarrel. The black saw this man enter the hiding place the day before yesterday, and he says that he can guide us to it."

"That will do, sub-inspector. You may stand down." The Sub-inspector left the witness-box, having said rather more than he intended to say, and Dunphy, in his broadcloth suit, with his beaver on the bench beside him, realised that it had been well worth his while to run the risk of attending the trial.

He waited until the end, and heard his Honor's impressive remarks while sentencing Rogers and Warburton to five years' penal servitude apiece.

"A very just punishment, as I take it, sir," said Dunphy to the old gentleman who sat beside him, but to his astonishment the old gentleman burst into a violent tirade against all judges and all courts whatsoever.

"None calleth for justice," he thundered, "nor any pleadeth for truth; they trust in vanity, and speak lies, they conceive mischief and bring forth iniquity. Their feet run to evil, and they make haste to shed innocent blood. The way of peace they know not, and there is no judgement in their goings."

"Or-rder in the coort ! " thundered a strident voice from the door, and Dunphy hurried away from a neighbourhood which was attracting curious glances from all the spectators, and which threatened to be more conspicuous than was either desirable or safe for him.

He found his horse where he had tied him up outside the courthouse, and as he mounted with the deliberateness proper to the head of an important financial institution he heard an excited passer-by shout to a friend on the other side of the street:

"Hi! Bill, have you heard the news. Jack Dunphy is in town. Bishop Troughton's groom saw a man riding in this morning, and recognised the horse at once. It was the identical animal that Dunphy stole from the bishop."

"Why didn't they catch him, the !" Bill shouted back.

"Unfortunately the bishop's groom lost sight of the horse when he came into town, and now he's too drunk to be able to tell the difference between a horse and a cow. But the police are on the look-out for Dunphy. It's any odds that they will nab him this time."

"Oh, is it?" muttered Dunphy between his teeth. He shook up his horse, and headed away for distant Mount Elephant without experiencing the slightest interference from anyone.

But late in the afternoon there was an exciting scene at the Bathurst lock-up. A crowd of fully a thousand people were gathered outside, and loud cheers were raised when some irresponsible person announced: "They've arrested another bushranger! They've got Jack Dunphy."

Everybody struggled to get nearer to the door of the lock-up in order to have a peep at the notorious outlaw, and several estimable citizens of Bathurst had their toes badly trampled on, and their clothes torn in the struggle.

Inside the lock-up stood Constable Mahoney, with a light of victory in his eyes at last, and his leg-of-mutton fist firmly clenched on the collar of a dilapidated brown coat, full of holes. The coat was worn by a man with a black beard. He also wore a nondescript hat and a pair of very dirty moleskins, tucked into high boots. He was incoherent, indeed almost speechless, with rage.

"I wuz ridin' t'roo the bush whin I seen him skulkin' along near the thrack," said Mahoney to Senior-constable Lugg, in charge of the lock-up. "Shure, I reckernised him at wanst. I cud take my Bible oat' to that ould brown, holey coat, an' the hat wid the piece out of it, an' them dhurty moleskin breeches. Didn't I see 'em all close enough to me whin he charged me down an' galloped over me beyant at Bottlebrush Flat."

"I'll have you discharged from the force for this outrage," shouted the infuriated prisoner. "I was going up to you to report the assault committed upon me on the public road when you jumped off your horse and actually put handcuffs on me. Do you know who I am, sir ~"

"Faix, I know who ye are well enough, Jack Dunphy," retorted

Mahoney, "an' I'm going to lock ye up here for the night, an' ye'll come befure the Binch in the mornin'."

Without another word he hustled his prisoner down a long passage, with gloomy little cells opening off it on either side, and shoved him into one of the cells, banging the door, and turning the key on him. The enraged prisoner hammered in vain on the door of his cell. In vain, also, he bestowed maledictions upon the absent constable, who proceeded to relate the story of the arrest triumphantly to the knot of police and newspaper reporters who quickly gathered at the scene.

It was not until ten o'clock next morning that Mr. Binge, the police-magistrate, who occupied the bench, discovered, with horror, that the alleged bushranger, who was brought before him as Jack Dunphy, was no other than the influential manager of his own bank, Mr. Robert Pinkie, of Evergreen Hall, Darling Point, Sydney.

It required many and abject apologies on the part of Mahoney before Mr. Pinkie consented to withdraw his demand for the trooper's dismissal.

By common consent, Esther and David avoided all reference to the topic of Morosini's death when left alone by Dunphy. But though they never spoke of it, they were always thinking of it.

To Esther, fresh from her quiet Cornish home, the events of the last few weeks were full of grotesque horror. Things unimaginable had occurred. Events that seemed no more real than the grisly phantasmagoria of delirium had gone through the hollow form of taking place. Was she herself, that silent, haggard being in boots and breeches and Crimean shirt, in very truth that same Esther Pennycuick whose childhood was spent in picking daisies by an English stream, and whose happy girlhood was passed on a farmstead looking out over the grey waters of the Channel, with lowing cattle in the byre, and a stern-faced old father poring over his Bible in the cottage on the hill! She could scarcely believe it possible.

The dreadful, tongueless, red-haired man looking at her with his questioning eyes, and always brooding upon blood¬shed and vengeance, appalled her soul. . The spirit of that passion-ridden Italian, whose flame of life was snuffed out in a second, seemed to stand between David Venn and herself. And, then, there was David, who loved her, and whom she loved. He was separated from her by a barrier that she had herself erected, and that she feared to break down now, lest seeing it, he should turn from her with loathing.

"And yet it had to be," said Esther to herself, glancing at David, who was staring into the log fire, and at the Red Cobber, who regarded her with a malignant glance that seemed to read her very thoughts. If the Red Cobber ever found out that she had befriended the black who had done him such bitter, irremediable evil, he would be quite capable of including her in his vengeance. Esther realised that quite clearly, and she shivered.

David Venn, for his part, had much to think of as he sat staring into the log fire. His love for Esther had never wavered. But the idea that the stain of blood - however warrantably shed - was upon her hands haunted and oppressed him. He feared that he could never forget it. Gladly he had taken upon himself the guilt of the shooting - if guilt there really was in an act which hovered on the narrow boundary between unjustifiable homicide and justifiable self-defence. To save Esther from shame he would have done even more than that. But now it was borne in upon him that his assumption of the crime, though it might clear Esther in the eyes of the law, had not cleared her in his eyes, and, apparently, had not cleared her in her own. He felt the invisible bar between them daily more and more. And evidently she felt it too, if he could judge by her haggard face and conscience-stricken manner.

"By heavens, you're not a particularly cheerful crew for a man to come home to," said Dunphy, boisterously, as he made his way through the narrow tunnel, leading the big brown horse behind him, on the day after his hurried departure from Bathurst.

David Venn, Esther, and the Red Cobber said nothing ¬the first two because they had nothing to say, and the last because he would never say anything again to anybody.

The bishop's horse had already made himself quite at home in his lawless surroundings. He had his own place, and bundle of hay, next to his mate, who now belonged to David Venn, and further along in the tunnel was the Red Cobber's big thoroughbred, formerly, as the advertisements would say, "the property of a gentleman" namely, old Montgomery

A smart grey pony, that Dunphy had lifted out of a paddock near Bottlebrush Flat, was the mount provided for "Jack" Pennycuick.

"We're goin' to be busy here shortly," said Dunphy to Venn, "and, as your neck is in as much danger as mine, on account of that little job of yours down at the Turon, I reckon you'd better take notice. Tallard has found out where we are."

David Venn's heart gave a leap. So he would be recaptured after all - unless, with Dunphy's assistance, he could again escape. "How did Tallard find out?" he asked.

"One of the black-trackers told him," said Dunphy. "It seems that the black was stalking Darby Kennedy here, and saw him entering the mouth of the tunnel." Then turning to the Red Cobber, he shot a wrathful glance at him. "Nice kind of fool you must be, too," he added, bitterly, "to let a blackfellow catch you like that. You've given the whole show away."

The Red Cobber's face was distorted by a spasm of rage and hate, all the more expressive 'because of his inability to speak. It was one more count in his long indictment against his enemy, Jacky.

"Well, we've got to get ready for a siege, that's all," said Dunphy, grimly. "I'm not going out of here to be caught and laid by the heels in Bathurst Gaol. If they want me, they'll have to come here for me, and it will take them all their time to get me."

"When is Tallard likely to come?" asked David Venn, almost glad that a crisis was at last approaching.

"Shouldn't wonder if he gets here by daybreak," said Dunphy, "and he has got twenty mounted troopers with him. He'll come at us from the east end of the tunnel, because that's the entrance that Darby always uses. The black-tracker must have seen him going into it. Tallard cannot know that the tunnel goes through into the other valley, and he doesn't know that it has an opening screened by bushes at the top on the flank of the mountain. That's how we'll get him. Come along now. We have to get out of this."

"But what for?" asked Venn, who had no idea of the scheme that had framed itself in Dunphy's brain.

"To block the tunnel," said Dunphy, "and hold them back on the east side, while we get away on the west. You'll see presently."

17

A Duel in the Mist

DUNPHY led the way out of the tunnel, after directing Darby Kennedy to bring a pick-axe and a coil of rope. David Venn and Esther followed. The whole four climbed the steep side of the mountain by a practicable route that the Red Cobber had discovered during his frequent ramblings on the look-out for Jacky.

It took them one full hour of hard climbing before they reached the saddle, which was split in two by the narrow gorge that formed the tunnel. This saddle, or plateau, was strewn with huge boulders. The live scrub that covered the opening into the gorge from the top was of uneven density. In some places it was thick and impenetrable. In others it was thin, letting in ample light and air to the occupants who made their home and refuge five hundred feet below.

There was bright moonlight on the plateau, and Dunphy examined the granite boulders with close attention.

The Red Cobber, who had grasped Dunphy's idea, pointed to a huge monolith standing only a few yards from the screened opening.

"No good, Darby," cried Dunphy. "Too big. She'd stick half way down, an' we'd be done."

He scrutinised the boulders closely, and at last fixed on one suitable for his plan. It was a rough oblong, weighing about a ton.

"This one will do finely," said Dunphy.

It was a long job to shift the boulder from its position into a spot at the extreme edge of the narrow opening into the gorge, but by dint of levering it with stout branches the task was at last accomplished.

Peering down through the leafy thatch of light scrub that formed the roof of the tunnel, Dunphy could see the fire burning brightly five hundred feet below him. The fire marked the position of the domicile in the tunnel. Dunphy selected a spot a few yards further to the west side.

"Here we are," he said. "Reckon we won't do any better than this."

Esther Pennycuick, wondering whether it was really she herself or some 'stranger who had invaded her personality, pulled and pushed with the three men on the lonely and silent mountain plateau. Little by little the huge oblong was slowly levered into its assigned position at the extreme edge of the opening, which was roofed at that spot with twigs and leaves.

Dunphy levered it the last few inches by himself, judging the width of the boulder carefully, so that it over-hung the opening considerably without falling in.

"That's it exactly," he grunted with satisfaction. The Red Cobber looked at him inquiringly.

"Now, Darby," said Dunphy. "This is your job, and take care that you don't make a mess of it. Venn and the boy and I will stand 'em off as long as we can, but we'll have all the horses at the western end of the tunnel. If Tallard and the troopers break through that's the time for you to act. By looking down you will be able to see where they are. Before the foremost of them reaches the house in the middle let her go. I reckon that lump of granite will go down through the spilt in the rock like a bullet through a gun barrel. It will choke up the tunnel so thoroughly that nobody will ever get through it without blasting away the boulder. As soon as you've dropped her make the best of your way to meet us on the west side. We'll have your horse ready for you, and I judge that we'll be a hundred miles away before Tallard finds out which way we've gone. We'll hit Bell's Line, and be down on the Hawkesbury before he is out of the eastern valley."

The Red Cobber grinned with delight and took up his position beside the granite boulder. He peered down through the bushes and saw the log fire burning far below him, a few paces to the eastward. He declined to return with the others to the tunnel. Taking a hunk of bread and a lump of meat from his pocket, he devoured them like a ravenous dog, and then prepared to keep vigil till daybreak.

Dunphy, David Venn, and Esther returned to the tunnel, and crouched over the bright fire, for the night was cold. As they warmed themselves in the glow of the burning wood, Dunphy related the full story of his visit to the Bathurst court-house, chuckling heartily at his own audacity. He told them also of the old man who sat next to him on the bench at the back, and who interlarded his conversation freely with Scriptural texts.

Esther gave a convulsive start. "What was the old man like?" she asked, with carefully repressed vehemence.

"His face looked as if it had been chopped out of a block of red gum with an axe," replied Dunphy, "his mouth was like a steel trap, an' he had blazing eyes, about the same colour as your own."

Esther recognised the description at once. It was that of her father, without a doubt. He had been brought to Bathurst by the police to give evidence against David Venn for the murder of Morosini. As soon as David was captured the police would confront him with old Malachi, and out of her father's mouth the fatal evidence would have to come that might hang her lover for a deed of which he was innocent. The girl shivered as she looked into the fire.

Dunphy flung himself down on the pile of skins in the corner and heavy snores soon proclaimed that he was no longer a listener.

"Do not be afraid, dear," said David, " I'll take care of you, and I'll see that the police do not take you." He murmured under his breath the old refrain that brought back a memory of the camp fires on the Turon, and the distant voice that used to sing;-

"And for bonnie Annie Laurie I'd lay me doon an' dee."

But David Venn did not put his arms round the girl.

. There was a trace of restraint in his emotion; an icy touch of mistrust at his heart. He realised it himself. The thought that Esther had blood on her hands made him recoil instinctively from her, although his whole nature craved for her. it was the very paradox of passion.

And Esther realised it, too, and with the infallible intuition of woman, she understood it at once. He is turning from me, she said in her inmost heart. He loves me still - enough to give his life for me, but he shrinks from the idea of wedding a woman who has killed a man. Oh, what shall I do? What. shall I do?

Far through the night the unhappy pair sat in front of the log fire, looking into the embers and occasionally talking in low tones of the attack that was expected in the morning. Jack Dunphy, who did not know the meaning of disquietude in the presence of danger, snored peacefully on his rude bed of skins.

But outside, on the plateau far above their heads, the Red Cobber kept his ceaseless vigil. He strode up and down the plateau, passing and repassing the boulder placed on the edge of the open gap, below which were the three occupants of the house in the tunnel.

At last, looking eastwards across the endless expanse of rolling ranges, he saw the first brilliant streaks that heralded the coming day. The rosy colour had broadened out and turned all those towering bush-clad solitudes into ramparts of fairyland.

But what was that below the towering ramparts? Every valley was filled with rolling billows. Had the ocean, then, broken in and flooded the country? Had some great tidal wave flowed in from the Pacific and inundated New South Wales? A stranger might have thought so, but this dumb, red-haired giant, leaning on his hardwood club upon the plateau of Mount Elephant, was familiar with the beautiful phenomenon. It was the morning mist that poured through all the valleys, submerging the whole country except the tops of the ranges, which projected like islands from the sea.

The Red Cobber had seen that wonderful sight many times before - the sea of billowing vapor extending on every side, and stained to blood - colour by the beams of the rising sun. But he looked at it uneasily this time - and vaguely wondered whether he would ever see it again. What deadly forces might not be hidden in the depths of that sea of rosy vapor which was coming down the eastern valley so fast, and would soon envelop even the plateau of Mount Elephant itself?

Ah, it had arrived already.

The Red Cobber groped his way through the mist to the side of the great boulder that had been dragged to the edge of the sheer descent into the narrow cleft in the mountain side where Jack Dunphy had made his city of refuge. There the Red Cobber took his stand, knowing that if he moved from it he would lose himself. Chilled to the bone by the enfolding mist, the Red Cobber waited with what patience he could muster for the coming of the expected enemy. How would that enemy come?

The mist closed down on the valley through which Sub-inspector Tallard was riding at the head of his twenty troopers, to attack the stronghold of Jack Dunphy. The detachment was led by the blackboy, Jacky, who acted as guide. Jacky was mounted, and Jimmy, his mate, rode beside him.

Slowly the troopers rode through the dense mist, those behind calling at intervals to the leaders in order to make sure of their position. Tallard had made a start at midnight, so as to reach the gorge soon after daybreak. The men rode in single file, each trooper being able to see no further than the tail of the horse in front of him and sometimes not even that.

Arriving at the base of Mount Elephant, Jacky held a brief conversation with Jimmy in their unknown tongue. He told his mate the lie of the country, and indicated. the position of the opening of the narrow cleft in the mountain. Then he drew up alongside Tallard.

"Mine tinkit findem hole in rock bimeby plenty soon," he muttered. "Jacky go now. Jimmy stay alonga boss; findem hole." The blackboy slipped off his horse, handed the bridle to his mate, and disappeared in the dense mist. In his previous wanderings he had explored the mountain thoroughly, and had discovered the opening screened with foliage at the top of the cleft. It seemed to Jacky that the top of the cleft needed watching. He began to scramble up the mountain side with the agility of a; native-cat.

The Red Cobber, standing by the boulder poised on the edge of the opening, knew not that his deadliest enemy was approaching under cover of that chilling and impenetrable mist.

In the house in the tunnel, the log-fire burned low.

Dunphy awoke, rubbed his eyes, and leaped to his feet.

"Tallard and his men will be here soon, I reckon," he muttered. "Better have a look at the horses, Venn. They are just outside the tunnel, in the western valley. We may need 'em soon. if the troopers are too many for us to stand 'em off."

So David Venn left the fire, with Esther still sitting in front of it, and groped his way to the western end of the tunnel to see that the horses were safe. It took him some time to find them in the mist. Dunphy and Esther remained by the fire, which was about eighty yards from the eastern opening of the cleft.

Stealing through the mist, Jacky, the blackboy, climbed swiftly to the plateau, and finding himself on level ground, felt his way cautiously to the edge of the longitudinal cleft.

Very soon he saw a big boulder looming up in front of him. Jacky was puzzled. The boulder certainly was not there when he explored the place a few days previously. He dropped on his stomach and crawled cautiously forward. Ha! There was a man standing beside the boulder. Jacky could see the man dimly. Something in the pose and outline of that gigantic figure struck a familiar note. Then, in a flash, the truth came home to Jacky. It was the Red Cobber. The huge figure was shrouded in the mist, but there was no mistaking it.

The Red Cobber found himself staring through the mist at a dark log on the ground, where a few minutes before there had been no log. He scratched his head doubtfully.

All at once the log up-ended itself from the ground and precipitated itself upon the Red Cobber. He uttered a horrible guttural cry of alarm as two powerful black arms were twined around his body.

Darby Kennedy realised that he was in the grip of his foe.

The Red Cobber had his sheath knife at his belt, and he strove furiously to use it, but his arms were pinioned, and he could not reach it. Jacky shifted his grip with his right hand and sought his enemy's throat. The Red Cobber got one arm free, and dealt the black a smashing blow with his fist. As the black fell, he pulled his enemy with him, and buried his white teeth in the Red Cobber's throat. Over and over on the rough ground rolled the white man and the black, locked in a death grip.

The Red Cobber's sinewy fingers closed like a vice upon the black-tracker's windpipe. Jacky gurgled, and let go the hold with his teeth, to snap his powerful jaws again upon the hand that was choking him. The Red Cobber held on though the blackboy's teeth were meeting in his hand.

So, enfolded in the mist, the Caucasian and the primitive

fought with teeth and claws, according to the age-old habit of the creatures from whom they sprang. Minutes passed, arid still they gripped and tore in a wordless fury, for it was a fight to the death.

Ha! The Red Cobber was uppermost at last. With his knee on the blackboy's chest he wrenched his wounded left hand free, and with his right hand he seized his enemy's throat in a surer grip. He had him at last. The end was not far off. The blackboy's eyes were starting from their sockets. As the Red Cobber drew back his wounded hand he felt the great rocky boulder beside him.

But Jacky was not yet done with. Making a supreme effort, he arched his back as he lay on the ground, and displaced the knee that was crushing in his breastbone. The Red Cobber gave a lurch, though he still retained his grip of the blackboy's throat.

The lurch threw the Red Cobber's whole weight against the mighty boulder, which was poised on the edge of the opening in the mountain's flank. The boulder swayed - tottered - and fell.

And the two men, still locked in their mutual death-grip, fell with it.

With a crashing and rending of leaves and branches, the monolith burst through the interlacing foliage that formed the roof of the immense tunnel, and, thundering down from a height of five hundred feet, fell with an earth-shaking thud into the narrow passage, and completely blocked it up, some half-a-dozen yards on the western side of the burning logs that formed Jack Dunphy's hearth fire.

The mangled remains of the two men who had fallen with the boulder lay on the floor of the tunnel beside the boulder on the further side from Dunphy and Esther, who stared at each other speechlessly for a few moments.

18

The Last Stand

DUNPHY was the first to recover the use of his wits. "Well, my lad," he said, "that was narrow shave for us, and no mistake. Wonder what made Darby shove her over like that without a word of warning."

Esther was trembling all over. "David! David!"was all she could say.

"That cursed fool of a Darby has blocked our escape," said Dunphy, bitterly. "We're cut off from David, and from the horses, too. I reckon this is goin' to be Jack Dunphy's last fight, my lad. There's only one way out of this trap now, and that is forward, through the troopers. You stay here while I go to the mouth of the tunnel, and see if the way is clear. I'm afraid it isn't, for Darby wouldn't have pushed the stone over unless. something had happened up above there." He disappeared into the dark passage that had its exit into the eastern valley, and Esther remained by herself, trembling.

"Jack, are you there?" It was David's· voice speaking.

He was on the other side of the boulder that blocked the tunnel.

"Yes, David, I am here," said Esther faintly. " Dunphy has gone to the mouth of the tunnel, and I am all alone. Oh, David, what shall we do?"

"Listen, little girl," said David, "I see a chance of getting you away safely, even now, and I'm going to try it. I will ride round to the gap; it's only five miles away, and come through into the valley where the troopers are. I think I can draw them off, for when they see me they will think that we have all got out. I reckon they're sure to hunt me, and if they do, then you and Dunphy can come out of the tunnel and climb back over the plateau down to the horses. If I get away, I'll make back to the Red Cobber's hut, looking down on the Turon, and wait for you there. You and I will get away to Sydney then. Keep up your pluck, little girl. I must go now, for there is no time to lose. And, Esther - "

"Yes, David."

"If anything happens to me, remember me always dear, for the sake of the old days, and go back to your father on the Turon. The police will never trouble you again, for I shall take your secret with me.'"

Her secret, her secret! Esther could hardly speak for tears. If David only knew - if he only knew!

"Good-bye, David," she sobbed. "Good-bye. You're the bravest man I ever heard of, and the best."

David Venn looked down at his feet, and, in horror, saw the dead bodies of Jacky and the Red Cobber. Next moment he was gone.

When Dunphy came back, Esther told him of David's plan. "Too late, I'm afraid," grunted Dunphy. "He'll never get there in time. They're on us now. Where's my gun?"

He seized the short-barrelled rifle that stood against the rock near his pile of rugs, and she handed him the powder flask and the bag of bullets. "You stay here," he commanded, " and don't come out until I call you. A lad like you didn't ought to be in a fix like this at all."

Jack Dunphy, who seldom wasted sentiment upon anybody, had a kindly feeling for the lad whom Venn had brought into the gang - an inexplicable kindly feeling for which he could in no way account. He had told himself a dozen times a day that he was a fool to have a useless lad like that hanging around, yet he had never taken the decisive step of dismissing him. And now Jack Dunphy was going to stand in the mouth of the tunnel and hold it against the little regiment of troopers. "And all for the sake of that blamed boy," he grumbled to himself, "I'm sure I don't know why I -"

"Dunphy, I call upon you, in the Queen's name, to surrender," shouted a harsh voice far away. "I know where you are, and I intend to take you alive or dead."

"Oh, that's it, is it?" muttered Dunphy. He ran forward towards the mouth of the tunnel to see if he could locate the enemy. Jimmy had halted the detachment at a point about fifty yards to the left of the tunnel.

It was a splendid shot, considering that he had never been there himself before, and had nothing but Jacky's information to go on. Still, he had only scored an "outer." He had not hit the bull's-eye.

It was now half-past six o'clock in the morning, and the white, billowy mist still filled the valley from end to end. It would not rise for another hour, at least. When Dunphy looked out from the mouth of the tunnel he could see nothing. But his keen ear detected low voices not far away.

Quickly he became aware that some of the troopers had dismounted, and were groping with their hands along the face of the rock to find the narrow cleft that Jacky had described. They seemed to be on his right. It was evident that the challenge of the Sub-inspector was a "bluff," since the location of the tunnel was not discovered when he called upon Dunphy to surrender.

At that moment it flashed through Dunphy's mind that he might escape even then. The valley ran approximately north and south, and the troopers were to the south of him. If he slipped away through the dense mist, before they found the opening of the tunnel, and then headed north, he could not be caught. But it would have to be done at once. There was no time to run back for his companion in the tunnel, and it was impossible to call out, for the sound of his voice would bring up the searching troopers at once.

Just for a moment Dunphy hesitated. Then he stamped his foot. "No, I'm - if I will," he muttered. "I'll not be such a cur as to leave the lad inside there alone."

Another thought had struck him. There might yet be time for the lad Pennycuick to slip away through the mist. "I'll stay an' fight for the old home," he murmured to himself, "for if I left it they'd get me mighty soon, but it's different with the lad."

He rushed back, grasped Esther by the hand, and dragged her to the mouth of the tunnel. "Out you go young chap," said Dunphy. "They'll never see you in this blessed rain cloud. Don't turn round, or you'll lose yourself for sure. Keep straight up the valley, and the mist will rise in another hour. Then make for the Gap, and double back to Darby Kennedy's place. I reckon you'll find Darby there, and he'll give you some tucker. Take my advice and go back to the Turon.

So long." He shoved her out into the mist, and turned her towards the left. The mist swallowed her up, and Dunphy saw her no more.

But, feeling their way slowly along the rock-face he saw the foremost of the troopers. They were within fifteen yards of him. He retreated hastily into the tunnel, and took cover behind one of the natural buttresses that projected at intervals into the gradually widening passage.

Ah! They had found the entrance at last!

"Come out and surrender, Dunphy. The game is up."

It was Tallard's voice that spoke.

The only reply was a flash, a bang, and a bullet singing into the mist. Dunphy had thrown himself down on the ground, and had fired from behind the buttress, exposing only the top of his head and one eye.

The troopers hastily retired behind the angle of the rocky wall in which Nature had cloven the passage. Tallard was non-plussed. "There are probably three or four of them in there," he said to Mitford, "and if we rush them there is bound to be heavy loss of life."

"What about giving them a volley?" suggested Mitford. Tallard was, doubtful, but at last consented. He insisted, however, that the men inside the tunnel, whoever they were, should be challenged first. The challenge was given, but there was no reply. A dozen troopers formed up in the mist, and fired at the word of command into the tunnel. Before the reverberations had died away. there was an answering flash in the tunnel, and one of them - it was Trooper Beggs - fell to the ground with a bullet through his thigh. Tallard grew worried.

A black visage loomed through the dense vapor. "Mine bin tinkit findcm hole up a top." This was the reasoned conclusion of Jimmy, and Tallard wondered why he himself had not thought of it before. So Jimmy set out to climb to the plateau, which was split transversely by the deep and narrow chasm in which Dunphy had made his domicile, and the troopers drew off from the opening to await the black-tracker's report.

It was then that disaster came to Esther Pennycuick.

Groping her way through the dense white vapor that filled the valley, she had inadvertently turned right round. Terrified by the sound of the firing, and completely misjudging the position of the troopers, she ran right into them. Trooper Mahoney saw a woebegone little figure moving aimlessly through the mist, and at once stretched out a brawny arm and gripped it.

"Come along here, young felly, till I hov a luk at ye," he said, and then, in great astonishment "Begob, if it ain't ould Malachi Pennycuick's bye I'm a Dutchman, Howja yet here, me son?"

So Esther confessed that she had escaped from the tunnel, and that Dunphy, the leader of the gang, was still in there. Mahoney, who was duly impressed with the sense of his own importance, and who was at the same time greatly mystified at finding this quiet and well-behaved lad in the company of the desperate bushranger, handed Esther over to Sub-inspector Tallard, who cross-examined her severely about her connection with the gang, and received very unsatisfactory replies to his questions. She was placed in charge of Mahoney, and Tallard warned her that any attempt to escape would be visited with the most serious consequences.

Soon after seven o'clock the mist vanished from the valley, dispelled by the rays of the sun, and with the ebbing of the tidal sea of white, billowy vapor, Tallard saw for the first time the nature of the country that he was in.

A wide and winding valley, thickly clad with light timber, was bounded on one side by Mount Elephant, which merged into the lower ranges adjoining it, and on the other side by precipitious, rocky cliffs, which were quite unclimbable. It was no easy task even to ride north or south through the timbered valley into which the narrow chasm in the flank of Mount Elephant opened. A difficult place to find, truly and but for the private peregrinations of Jacky, the black-tracker, the probability was that it would never have been discovered.

The troopers gathered in little knots well at the side of the opening. Occasionally one of them would stick his helmet on the end of his rifle barrel, and project it cautiously round the corner of the opening. Instantly the report of a rifle followed from the depths of the chasm, and the helmet was withdrawn with a bullet through it.

Evidently Dunphy was not only unwounded, but very much alive.

Half an hour passed before Jimmy reached the plateau, and during all this time not a single trooper dared to show himself in front of the opening of the tunnel, much less enter it. The sight of Trooper Beggs, white-faced and groaning, with his thigh rudely bandaged, was an effective warning.

Mahoney stuck his helmet on a stick and shoved it beyond the edge of the wall of the tunnel so that it could be seen by anyone inside. There was no response. "Shure he's foxin' now," said Mahoney, and nothing could induce him to venture in himself.

A shout from Jimmy arrested the attention of the on-lookers below. "No can see white pfeller," he bellowed. "Him all gone." Jimmy had been peering down through the interlaced branches that grew over the top of the chasm. He could see the remains of the fire, and the huge boulder that completely blocked the passage, but he could not see Dunphy down below there. The black-tracker was puzzled by that boulder. Evidently it had been dropped down from above in order to block the passage. He could see where it had torn its way through the latticed leaves and twigs and branches beside him. The great hole was a convenient orifice through which to make his observations. But nobody was visible at the bottom of the chasm.

It occurred to Jimmy that the white pfeller who was being chased - for what reason he neither comprehended nor cared - had managed to climb over the boulder and get away through the tunnel, which, as he now saw for the first time, opened out into another valley beyond. But a close inspection of the barrier and of the smooth precipitous rock face on either side of it convinced Jimmy that it was insurmountable. Further away, towards the entrance of the tunnel, the walls were studded with projections and inequalities, but in the centre near the log-fire they were as smooth as glass. The disappearance of the "white pfeller" was unaccountable. Still" white pfellers" were an unaccountable people in Jimmy's experience. One never knew what they would do next.

Sub-inspector Tallard was chafing at the delay. He was trying to make up his mind to order order his men to rush the tunnel and capture

Occasionally a trooper would stick his helmet on the end of a rifle barrel.

when he happened to lift his eyes to the top of the chasm. What he saw there startled him. It was a bearded face, which rose through the leaves and twigs, interwoven to form the roof of the tunnel, five hundred feet above the level of the ground.

First the head emerged, and then the shoulders and arms. Tallard gazed at the apparition, too terrified to speak. Then he found his voice. "Look out, Jimmy," he yelled.

The bearded man seemed to rise out of the ground a score of paces from Jimmy, and he was on his feet on the solid plateau before Jimmy saw him. It was a marvellous effort. Dunphy had scaled the immense precipitous wall of the narrow chasm in the living rock for a height of five hundred feet, and had got out at the top.

He stood there, dazed for a few seconds by the brilliant sunlight, after being for so long immured in the gloom of the tunnel. And as he stood there Jimmy leaped at him. He might as well have leaped at a lion.

"Shoot it, men, what are you waiting for? Why don't you fire?" yelled Tallard, who was white with rage at the thought that the bushranger might even yet escape.

A dozen carbines were raised, and the irregular rattle, as the troopers aimed hastily and fired, echoed and re-echoed through the lonely valley, but Dunphy had heard Tallard's angry order. Seizing the black-tracker in his grip of steel, he held him in front of him as a shield, The round bullets buried themselves with a "phit-phit" in Jimmy's quivering body.

Hurling the corpse of the black into the chasm, Dunphy made his dash across the plateau, calculating that he would be out of range before the carbines could be re-loaded. But Tallard had still seven more carbines in reserve, not counting that of Trooper Beggs, the wounded man, and as Dunphy started to run, the Sub-inspector gave the order to fire.

Hard hit, the bushranger dropped on one knee on the rocky plateau. He had made a great bid for his life, and it was hard to lose it just when the way of escape was open. In a few more seconds he would have been over the ridge, and out of reach.

Kneeling on the ground with his chest shot all to pieces, Dunphy turned his face to the enemy, and shook his fist at the troopers.

"Ah, you dogs," he said, "I fought a dozen of you, but I couldn't fight a score."

Then he caught sight of Esther, who was crying bitterly. "Good-bye, Jack Pennycuick. Go back to your father my lad, and don't forget that I died game." A rush of blood and froth from the shattered lungs stopped his voice, and with a long gurgling sigh, he fell over in his death agony.

When the troopers reached the plateau he was dead.

Trooper Mitford peered down into the black depths of the chasm that Dunphy had climbed in search of freedom, and could not forbear a tribute of admiration. Looking down at the dead man's face, he said laconically, "Jack Dunphy, you were a scoundrel, but, by the Lord, you were a plucky one."

And that was Dunphy's only epitaph.

1 9

Driven to Bay

NOTHING prospered with Malachi Pennycuick after his daughter left him early on that morning in the past.

The young Scotsman, M'Lachlan, soon got tired of the fanatical old Cornishman, whose habit of muttering to himself was apt to get on the nerves of a listener. Even Martin Burke could not stand Malachi after Esther and David had gone away. He, too, departed, and joined some rollicking compatriots further up the river.

Then one day, while Malachi was working the cradle and his new partners were digging in the claim, some prowler visited his tent, and got away with the leather bag of gold dust and small slugs of gold that he had carefully planted. The old man became worse than ever after that. He began to talk to himself aloud. Guiseppe Bini watched him intently. It was evident to him that the old man with the evil eye was not quite right in the head. Bini reported the matter to the police camp, and urged that old Malachi should be placed under restraint. It was good policy on the part of Bini, since it was a mate of Bini's, one Giacopo Neri, who had robbed old Malachi's tent, and divided the spoil with Bini in return for valuable information. With the old man under lock and key, no evidence would be forthcoming against the enterprising pair.

So the police came and removed old Malachi to the police camp where he remained until an opportunity should occur of sending him to an asylum. Day after day he sat apart, muttering to himself, and nobody heeded him.

The matter stood thus at the Turon when Tallard and his troopers returned from the expedition to the bushranger's den at Mount Elephant. They brought with them Trooper Beggs, wounded, and Jack Pennycuick, a prisoner. Beggs received skilled medical attention from Dr. Herbert Curtis, formerly of St. Bartholomew's Hospital, London, but now a lucky digger at the Turon, and Jack Pennycuick was left in the care of Mahoney until the return of the Gold Commissioner, who had gone to Bathurst to confer with the District Superintendent with regard to the break-up of Dunphy's gang, and the hoped-for capture of the last member of it, one David Venn, who was still at large.

"All the others are accounted for are they, Mr. Grey?" inquired the District Superintendent, who sat at his office table, interviewing the visitor at the opposite side of it:

"I understand so from Tallard," said Mr. Grey, in his business-like tones. And then he proceeded to check off the ill-fated members of the gang on his fingers.

"There was the man who called himself Stanhope, and is believed to have been an English university man. He was shot at Bottlebrush Flat, and has since died of his wound. Then we have Warburton and Rogers, tried at the last Quarter Sessions, and each sentenced to five years with hard labour; Darby Kennedy, the ex-shepherd, employed by Mr. Montgomery, killed along with the black-tracker in falling from the top of the gorge; and Dunphy, the leader, shot by the police when he was on the point of making his escape. The only one still out, as far as I know, is David Venn, who is wanted for the murder of the Italian, Morosini."

"But Tallard says something in his report about a young boy being with the gang," said the District Superintendent, rummaging among his papers for the sub-inspector's report.

"Oh, yes, I had forgotten about him," said Mr. Grey.

"It's rather curious. He is a son of an old Cornish digger, named Malachi Pennycuick, with whom David Venn had a share in a river-frontage claim. I remember the lad perfectly well. I saw him in connection with a claim-jumping case. in which the Italian Morosini,

138

was the aggressor. In fact, it was the bad blood engendered by that incident which led up, I fancy, to the murder of the Italian. The boy disappeared from the goldfields soon after the escape of David Venn with the man Dunphy, who had apparently come down with the idea of carrying off the gold which was deposited with me for safe conduct under escort to Sydney. It never occurred to me that the boy had gone to join David Venn, but that is evidently what happened. I remember now that one of our black-trackers was missing for some days about that time. Young Pennycuick was on particularly friendly terms with him, and I fancy the blackboy must have helped him to find Venn. However, Jacky, the black-tracker, is dead now, and even if he were alive it would be impossible to get the truth out of him."

"Then this boy Pennycuick is still out with David Venn, I presume," said the District Superintendent, who was not very clear-headed, and had read Tallard's report very carelessly.

"No, no," replied the Gold Commissioner, "we have the boy safe in custody at the police camp at Golden Point. Tallard's men captured him when he was escaping through a dense mist shortly before Dunphy's desperate attempt to slip through the hands of the troopers."

"Then it's all plain sailing now," said the District Superintendent, with an air of relief. "The boy must know the whereabouts of David Venn. They were both in the den at Mount Elephant together, and it's Lombard street to a China orange that they arranged to meet at some rendezvous after getting away from the gorge. The question is -Where is that rendezvous?"

The Gold Commissioner had no idea where it was.

However, he would question the boy.

"You find out from the boy where that fellow Venn is hiding," said the District Superintendent, "and I'll send Tallard with a party of troopers to deal with him. You can take it from me that he won't escape again."

The District Superintendent put away his papers, and going to the cupboard, produced sherry and biscuits. After this light refreshment, the two officials chatted agreeably concerning the disturbed state of the country, and then the Gold Commissioner shook hands, and went out to his buggy and pair, that stood in the main street, with a mounted man on escort duty.

All the way to the Turon the Gold Commissioner found himself pondering on the very peculiar sequence of events that had occurred ever since the claim-jumping case that he had decided as between the old Cornish miner and that black-browed Italian.

There were things that Mr. Commissioner Grey found it very hard to understand. There were bits of evidence that could not be fitted together, turn and twist them how he would. Of course, it was perfectly natural for David Venn, after shooting the Italian in a moment of uncontrollable anger, to make his escape. But what was he doing with a loaded gun outside the tent at three o'clock in the morning?

And how did it come about that Morosini was there?

The dead man's statement to Dick Pentreath that he had got up and left his tent because he was afraid that David Venn would go there and shoot him, seemed very far-fetched. The more the Commissioner probed into David Venn's conduct the more inexplicable it seemed.

And then, after being tracked and captured asleep on Ponto Island, in the Macquarie River, and brought back to the Turon, David Venn had escaped again, But, how? He must have had assistance to enable him to release himself from the bullock-chain to which he was securely handcuffed. And Dunphy, also, must have had assistance. Who had helped them? Probably the boy, Pennycuick, who afterwards rejoined them.

It did not matter by what line of reasoning the Commissioner attacked the problem before him, he arrived invariably at the same "impasse." All lines led up to the boy Pennycuick. It was positively irritating. Mr. Grey decided to interrogate the boy Pennycuick the first thing in the morning.

The examination of the boy Pennycuick was conducted in the Commissioners' own office. Esther Pennycuick, dressed in her every-day garb, a thick Crimean shirt, moleskin trousers, tucked into high, heavy boots, with a blue handkerchief knotted round her sun-tanned neck, took her place in front of the Commissioner's table, and Mahoney stood beside her.

"Shurez av ye tell the trut' now, me bye, his 'Anner won't be too harrd on ye," whispered Mahoney, encouragingly, but his advice fell on unheeding ears. The truth! Ah, the truth was itself so monstrously improbable that Esther felt it must never be told at all. That was her mood when the interrogation began.

Mr. Grey was patient and determined. He began at the beginning. He elicited the story of "Jack" Pennycuick's arrival at the Turon with his father, and his meeting with David Venn. But the witness was plainly what lawyers call "hostile," and it demanded the utmost skill on the part of the examiner to extract any evidence at all.

Gradually and haltingly the witness confirmed by monosyllabic answers the story which was constructed by the Commissioner. Yes, she remembered the night of the 17th June. (Ah, yes, did she not remember it? - the camp fires, the starlight, and David Venn beside her, and the distant voice that was singing "Annie Laurie.")

Did the witness remember going to sleep that night in the tent along with old Mr. Pennycuick and David Venn? The witness did. (She remembered dreaming of David Venn, too, and how they walked together through a flower-strewn valley, and how a black snake, with cruel, glassy eyes, thrust out its head to strike at him, and how the terrified beating of her own heart awoke her.)

Could Jack Pennycuick recall hearing a shot fired in the night, and then seeing David Venn standing outside the tent with the smoking gun still in his hand, and looking down at the dead body of Morosini? "Jack" Pennycuick could remember it. (How, indeed, could she ever forget it? - that instantaneous impulse of the man who loved her, to take the deed upon his own shoulders - in order that she might go free.)

And so the examination proceeded, right down to the moment when she was captured by Mahoney in the mist that filled the valley, and blotted out the gigantic outline of Mount Elephant, and robbed her of freedom - and of David Venn.

But Mr. Commissioner Grey gave a sigh of great dissatisfaction. There was something wrong with the whole story. It did not ring true. That sulky boy opposite had lied to him. The Commissioner was convinced on that point. But why had he lied? Ah, that was the problem.

Again and again the Commissioner returned to his cross-examination. Again and again that pale, determined boy, with his monosyllabic replies, repeated different parts of the same story. A great deal of it was true - that was clear, because it was borne out by the evidence of the police. But the further the Commissioner pushed his examination the more he became convinced that a story in the main true, had been built upon some gigantic falsehood. What was the nature of that falsehood? He could not conjecture.

"Where is David Venn now?" The question was rapped out suddenly, but it achieved nothing. The witness did not know. And though it was passed with all the resource of a skilful cross-examiner, the witness did not falter. Esther thought, with a shudder, of the Red Cobber. She was prepared to suffer even the Red Cobber's terrible fate rather than disclose the hiding place of the man who loved her and sacrificed himself for her.

It was then that Mahoney contributed the one brilliant suggestion that marked his whole career in the police: "Av ye plaze, yer 'Anner," he said, "I'm thinkin' that maybe we might be afther findin' th' villian up at Darby Kennedy's hut."

Esther Pennycuick turned and shot a furious glance at Mahoney. The Commissioner intercepted the glance, and saw that Mahoney's chance bullet had hit the bull's-eye.

"Go and tell Mitford to come and see me at once," said the Commissioner to Mahoney. "We'll have the man who shot Morosini before the sun sets this evening."

And then Mr. Commissioner Grey, who had had some strange experiences in the course of his long and honorable official career, received the greatest surprise of his whole life.

"You need not trouble to send out your troopers," said the boy Pennycuick, who confronted the Commissioner with heaving chest and flashing eyes. "It was I who shot Morosini - and David Venn knows it."

20

A Night of Horror

WHEN David Venn at last rode through the Gap and entered the eastern valley, he found interminable miles before him. It was hard work getting through the timber, and although he pushed his horse to the utmost his progress was slow. His scheme for drawing off the troopers - and thus enabling Dunphy and Esther to escape broke down badly, for when he reached the entrance to the den all was deadly still. The police had disappeared. There was no sign either of Esther or of Dunphy.

David Venn realised that he was too late.

So he turned his horse's head, and rode back to the Gap, a prey to anxiety on behalf of Esther. Again and again he asked himself what had become of her. Was she wandering alone, lost in the ranges? Was she in the hands of the police? Was she dead? He went over the probabilities in each case until his brain reeled. And then he thought of Darby Kennedy, that dreadful, tongueless giant whose passion for revenge was sated at last, since he lay dead at the bottom of the mighty chasm, with his fingers still gripping the throat of his dead enemy.

It was evening before Venn came to the long strip of tussocky grassland that led up to the lonely and deserted hut formerly inhabited by the Red Cobber. He got a drink of water from the creek, but he was very hungry. His departure from the den had been so hurried that he came away without any food. He hoped to find some at the hut.

What an eerie place it was! He could see the hut in the distance on the edge of an open space, flanked by great boulders, a regular rampart, which concealed it from the view of any persons climbing the range out of the Turon valley. It was from that wall of boulders that the

Red Cobber had rolled down the rock that broke the leg of Jacky, the black-tracker, and led up to the aboriginal's terrible reprisal.

Shuddering in spite of himself, David rode up to the empty hut, and slid off his horse. He took off the saddle and bridle; then he hobbled the horse, and turned him loose to feed on the coarse grass. Entering the hut, David proceeded to make a search for food. A few mouldy biscuits, a piece of ancient cheese, and a couple of onions rewarded his investigation. He made a careful meal, reserving two biscuits and one of the onions until next day. If Dunphy and Esther did not arrive at the hut next day he determined to push on to Bathurst, and risk being recognised. To stay where he was meant starvation.

It was a fine, clear night, and Venn made up his mind to sleep in the open. Somehow, he could not fancy the notion of sleeping in Darby Kennedy's hut. It was in that hut that Jacky had done the terrible deed!

The horse, feeding quietly on the thick patches of coarse grass, was company for the man. He dropped off to sleep, and woke at sunrise, thanking heaven that the night was over at last. He had never been consciously superstitious, but the remembrance of the Red Cobber oppressed him. He saddled the horse, took a billy from the hut, and rode away to the creek, two miles off. Horse and man had a good drink, and David filled his billy. He scanned the country eagerly. No sign of Dunphy or Esther. He listened intently. Not a sound of bird or beast or human being broke the fearsome silence.

Back at the hut again, Venn devoured the last of the mouldy biscuits and the remaining onion. He unsaddled his horse and let him graze.

The day was long and the sun was hot. Venn was tormented with anxiety on account of Esther. He resolved to wait one more day. It would be terrible if she should arrive there and find only the deserted hut. So he walked up and down the grassy plateau, and at intervals talked to his horse, merely for the relief of hearing his own voice.

In the evening it began to rain. It was impossible to camp in the open air again. Reluctantly, the man entered the hut. There was a bunk, consisting of canvas nailed upon saplings at one side of the hut. Upon the floor, at the opposite side, was a pile of roughly-dressed wallaby skins.

Venn knew, without being told, that Jacky, with his broken leg, had lain upon the bunk, and that he had got up from it and dragged himself across the floor to stun the Red Cobber with a waddy, and then make him a mute for life.

Venn lay down on the skins and tried to sleep; but could not. Jacky and the Red Cobber were both dead. He had seen them himself locked in the last desperate grip, at the bottom of that mighty chasm in the rock. And yet he could almost swear that they were present in the hut with him.

He said to himself that he was probably light-headed from hunger. Yes, that must be the cause of his terrors. But was it possible that the hut was haunted? The thought recurred again and again, became.insistent, would not be repressed.

As the night wore on, and David Venn lay in, the haunted hut, listening to the beating of his own heart, invisible presences stalked beside him. When he kept his eyes open he could see nothing, but when he shut them the Red Cobber appeared, with cavernous, tongueless mouth wide open, with red hair and beard all matted with blood, and with eyes that had the green glare of the eyes of the starving dingo.

A cold sweat broke out on Venn. He would have moved. He would have got up and rushed from the hut, But he could not. His limbs refused their office,

The rain had cleared away, but the wind was rising.

It began to moan round the hut. It blew the door open. Venn did not care. He would not get up and shut it, since to do so meant that he would have to cross the floor where the unseen dead were-wrestling. He could almost see the black-tracker now dragging himself across the floor, in spite of his broken leg, to wreak his savage vengeance. In a moment he would bring his club down with a crash upon that huge red head. In another moment he would draw the knife from its sheath, and -

David Venn half raised himself on his elbow and stared out into the darkness of the hut. His breath came fast and thick. Those invisible presences would not be laid. His imagination, quickened by hunger and loneliness, reconstructed the whole scene.

And then a gruesome idea obsessed him. As he lay there on the Red Cobber's pile of rudely-dressed skins. it seemed to him that he had ceased to be David Venn, and had, in truth and in fact, become Darby Kennedy, the shepherd. On the bunk opposite, near the open door, lay Jacky, the black-tracker. He, Darby Kennedy, had rolled a rock down on Jacky, and had broken his leg. What would Jacky do? Perhaps he might be dangerous. It might be as well to get up and twist Jacky's neck. No, he would try to go to sleep again.

Ha! What was that? God! Something was moving in the hut, something real and terrifying. It was approaching the skins on which he lay. It was Jacky, the dead black-tracker, coming to stun him, and cut out his tongue. David Venn's tongue clove to his throat.

This was not imagination or idle, baseless terror. There was a dark form stealthily moving from the direction of the bunk towards the pile of skins. The thing that had been merely a nightmare had become real.

For David Venn, a lifetime of agony was concentrated into the next ten seconds. He saw a dark form crawling across the floor towards him. The figure rose when it reached the pile of skins. And then the dead man who had come to life again hurled himself upon his victim, and David Venn, in a frenzy of agony, felt himself being suffocated under the weight of a living body.

Next moment a pair of handcuffs clicked upon his wrists, and the voice of Trooper Mahoney said: "Begob, I got ye nice an' aisy, an' no. throuble at all, at all. So lave off gruntin', now, me boy, an' come along wid Mitford an' me back to the ould place; for the Commissioner won't ate his breakfast till he sees ye."

By the light of several lanterns, David Venn saw the troopers who had crowded into the hut behind Mahoney. They had brought food with them, and they generously shared it with their prisoner. David was himself again after eating, and, as the sun rose over the ranges, all the supernatural terrors of that awful night vanished.

One of the men mounted David's horse and rode away by the only practicable route, which was a wide detour, to the valley below. But the others descended the mountain on foot, taking their prisoner with them.

During the journey Mahoney told David the news. "Jack Dunphy is dead," he said, "the biggest villain that ever we seen in these parts, God rest his sowl. An' we have the' bye Pennycuick safe enough down at the police camp."

The heart of the prisoner leaped with thankfulness, and he pressed Mahoney for further information about the boy Pennycuick." So Esther had escaped, though Dunphy had been killed."

"Is the boy Pennycuick well?"

"He is that," said Mahoney, and then he abruptly cut off the supply of information. He remembered that the boy Pennycuick had confessed to shooting Morosini, though David Venn was the man charged with the crime. Mahoney made up his mind not to interfere with the intricacies of this case. He did not know which of them had shot Morosini, but he recollected having got into serious trouble himself up at Bathurst for charging, Mr. Robert Pinkie with being a bushranger. He intended to make no further mistakes of that kind. The Commissioner would probably give him another jacketing for talking too much to the prisoners. So he held his tongue.

Not another word could Venn extract from the trooper as he walked beside him back to the Turon.

After crossing the river, David passed the bullock-chain, stretched between the two trees. A new lot of drunks and disturbers of the peace were handcuffed to it, but Mitford was taking no more risks. He sent Venn straight up to the police camp, and left him under guard in the big tent until the Commissioner could deal with his case.

21

The Clouds Disperse

THE tent was divided into two parts by a canvas partition running the full length of it, and the compartment in which David was placed contained no furniture except a long table and a few chairs.

"I don't know what to be afther t'inkin' about," it, said Mahoney to his particular crony, Sandy M'Mickin, as the pair of them sat in their quarters cleaning their spurs, "for, I tell ye now, they've both confessed to me, an' tis a heavy load on me conscience, so it is. This mahn Venn confessed long ago, an' we tuk it down in ritin'. And now ye see the boy Pennycuick, he flings it out at the Commissioner as bowld as brass, that he done the shootin' himself. Mr. Gl'ey don't know which of 'em's the liar, an' no more don't I. But I reckon we'll find out by to-night. Ye'd better move the old looney, Sandy, me bye, for we'll be usin' the big tent to-night."

"A' richt, Mahoney. I'll just pit the auld body in the next compairtment." Sandy was always on the look-out for the easiest way of doing things.

So when Mr. Grey entered the big tent, and proceeded to examine David Venn, he had no idea that there was a profoundly interested listener just behind the partition. Malachi knew David's voice at once, and he listened, with his ear glued to the partition, to the startling tale that David unfolded.

"You say, then," said the Commissioner, " that you saw the outline of a man who was standing outside your tent, and that you fired at him and shot him through the tent, intending to kill him because you suspected him of plotting mischief against you."

"That is so, sir."

"You are aware, of course, that you had .no justification for such conduct, seeing that your life was not in danger, and that Morosini had a perfect right to be where he was."

"I thought that he intended to do some of us an injury."

"Well, Venn, you persist in sticking to this story, do you?"

"Yes, sir. I do."

"Would you. be surprised to hear that another person has confessed to the crime?"

Ah, that. was a staggerer! So Esther's nerve had deserted her, and she had owned up to the truth at last. David felt that all his sufferings had been in vain. He might as well have stayed on the claim with old Malachi, and let the law do its worst. He had just enough presence of mind, however, to reply that he was not aware that any other person had confessed to shooting Morosini. If so, that confession must have been made under some misapprehension.

"Fetch the boy Pennycuick here, Mahoney," said the Commissioner.

So Mahoney brought Esther in, and placed her at the table opposite David Venn. It was the first time that he had seen her since they parted in the tunnel just before the great boulder fell. It was the first time he had heard her voice since that farewell conversation, when they stood in the tunnel separated from each other by the barrier of the huge stone.

"Now, Pennycuick," said the Commissioner, sharply, "you have made a statement to me that it was you who shot the Italian, Pietro Morosini. Do you adhere to that statement?"

The answer "Yes, sir," came in a low voice that quivered with emotion.

"You admit that you took up the loaded gun, and deliberately shot and killed a man who was standing outside your tent, as he had a perfect right to do, and who had made no threats whatever against you ? "

" I do, sir," said Esther, almost in a whisper.

And then there came a voice - a deep and raucous voice - from behind the canvas partition which made David and Esther stare at each other in amazement, and caused the Commissioner himself to start up from his chair.

"Now, therefore," said the voice of the unseen speaker, "the Lord hath put a lying spirit in the mouth of those thy prophets. For a certain man of Belial came unto my house to spoil me, and behold I arose and slew him, yea, even as Amaziah did slay the Edomites. For I drew at a venture, and smote him between the joints of his harness, so .that he bowed down his head and died. The Lord do so to me, and more also, if I speak not the word of truth with my mouth in this matter."

"Bring that man in here at once," was the Commissioner's order to Mitford, and old Malachi was led in, trembling in a perfect fury of self-condemnation. He stretched out his hands towards Esther with a most pathetic gesture of appeal, but the strain was too much for "the boy Pennycuick." Esther fainted, and would have fallen to the ground if Mahoney had not caught her on his out-stretched arm.

"Take that boy outside, Mahoney," ordered the Commissioner, "and then ask Dr. Curtis, with my compliments, if he would be good enough to step round and attend to him."

When Esther had been taken out, old Malachi was given. a seat at the table, and, to the great astonishment of the Commissioner, he was able to give a detailed, consecutive account of all the events leading up to the shooting of Morosini. Cross-examination and re-examination failed to break down his straightforward story. He admitted that he had a grudge against Morosini. He explained that there was a small hole in the tent - close to the corner where he slept. Looking through this hole he saw and recognised Morosini. When the man came and stood close to the tent so that his eyes could be seen looking through another hole, he, Malachi Pennycuick, had snatched up the loaded gun and fired at him. He had never understood why David Venn took the crime upon his own shoulders.

The witness explained, however, that his conscience would not permit him any longer to keep silent. He was just beginning to quote some remarks by the prophet Habakkuk, which seemed to him to have a bearing on the subject, when a buzz of excitement was, heard at the door of the tent, and Mahoney pushed his way through the knot of constables and approached the Commissioner.

Standing close beside the Commissioner's chair, Trooper Mahoney raised his hand to his helmet in respectful salute, and said: "Av ye plaze, sor, Dr. Curtis's compliments, an' the boy Pennycuk is a gurl."

Although such a communication as that was enough to upset the equanimity of any tribunal of inquiry, Mr. Grey managed to keep his balance, and slowly and carefully he began to dig through the mass of puzzling contradictions that still remained in this case.

David Venn had flushed to the roots of his hair and had then turned deadly pale when Trooper Mahoney made his astounding communication. Mr. Grey began to have a faint inkling of the part of truth.

"Why did you assume the responsibility of the shooting of Morosini?" inquired the Commissioner, looking David Venn straight between the eyes.

"I cannot tell you sir," said David Venn.

So the Commissioner had to wait for the elucidation of the mystery until the boy Pennycuick, who was a girl, had sufficiently recovered to resume her evidence. She came back, still in her moleskins, high boots, and Crimean shirt, and still very pale, to face the ordeal of further examination.

The Commissioner, who began to have a glimmering idea of how the land lay, motioned to Esther to take her place next to David Venn. "Now," he said, "just tell me, my girl, in your own words, exactly the meaning of all this masquerading and mystification. In the first place, why have you been wearing boys' clothes ever since you came to the Turon ?"

"Because I wished to be with my father," said Esther, in a low voice, "to look after him. If I had worn girls' clothes I should not have been allowed to work on the field."

"Hum! And why did you tell me that it was you who shot Morosini?"

"Because I did not wish David Venn to be thought guilty of that act," and then almost in a whisper, "David thought it was I who fired the shot, which I saw my father fire. That was the reason why David snatched up the gun and pretended to have done it himself."

"But you allowed him to remain under that mis-apprehension?"

"Yes."

"Why?"

"Because I wanted to save my father. I was in a terrible predicament. David Venn made his escape in the first place before I knew what he had done. I realised that he had drawn away suspicion from my father upon himself. I knew that as long as he was at liberty my father was safe from the police, and so even when he had been recaptured the first time I allowed him to go on thinking that he was taking my crime upon his shoulders. My father's liberty - perhaps his life - was at stake. He could not escape and maintain himself in the bush, he was too old. I loved my father, and so -and so- I lied to David Venn - that is all. I let him think that he was saving me by going out and joining the bushrangers. There was no reason why he should have done it to save my father. He did it because - because he loved me. And now I suppose he - he hates me."

nd so the truth came out at last, and Esther Pennycuick, in her moleskins and Crimean shirt, placed her arms upon the table and sank her head between them and was shaken by a storm of womanly sobs.

Mr. Commissioner Grey thought for about half a minute harder than he had ever thought in his life.

Then he pronounced his decision. "You, Venn, and you, Miss Pennycuick, are discharged. It is plain to me that the old man here, whose intellect is now unhappily failing, is alone responsible for the shooting of the Italian. As for your association with Dunphy and the other bushrangers, I prefer to regard it as to a large extent involuntary, believing as I do that neither of you had any evil intent in what you did. Malachi Pennycuick will be cared for, but will be kept under supervision during Her Majesty's pleasure. You, the other two, may go."

The Commissioner gathered up his papers and left hastily. Esther went up to her father and kissed him on the forehead. Then she looked sadly at David. "Can you forgive me?" she said.

David Venn clasped her by the hand. "Dear little girl," he said, "you know that I have always loved you. Do you think I could love you any the less because you tried to save your father 1 I know now that the old man was not responsible for what he did, and I am pretty sure, too, that Morosini more than half deserved what he got. At the same time I cannot help feeling truly thankful that this little hand of yours is free from the stain of blood. That knowledge rewards me for everything Esther, my darling, you and I have gone through too much together to be divided ever again."

As the man and the girl walked out together towards the camp-fires burning near the tents they heard the same mellow tenor in the distance singing the same song - the song which seemed to have moulded their lives. Looking into each other's eyes they heard from far away up the valley, the we'll remembered lines:-

> Maxwellton's braes are bonnie
> Where early fa's the dew ~
> An' 'twas there that Annie Laurie
> Gied me her promise true;
> Gied me her promise true,
> Which ne'er forgot shall be,
> And for bonnie Annie Laurie
> I'd lay me doon an' dee.

www.ingramcontent.com/pod-product-compliance
Lightning Source LLC
Chambersburg PA
CBHW031312280626
47169CB00018B/1250